Wild Desire

Wilder Irish, book two

Mari Carr

ISBN: 978-1-950870-12-7

Editor: Kelli Collins

Cover artist: Melissa Gill Designs

Print formatting: Mari Carr

Dedication

This book is dedicated to Lila Dubois.
The queen of *Top Chef*-style writing sprints.
"Time's up! Hands off the keyboard!"
Without her tireless spirit, intense bullying, and inspirational lake house music,
February Stars quite simply wouldn't be the same story.

It's better…because of her…and her insanity.

Also—extra thanks to Lila for allowing me to use a version of her daughter's name for my heroine.
Pronunciation   is   A-LISH

Prologue

"Ailis, love. Are you okay?"

Patrick's tiny redheaded granddaughter stood by the side of his bed, tears in her big blue eyes.

"I had a bad dream. Mommy and Daddy aren't back yet."

Patrick's daughter Teagan and her husband, Sky, were performing tonight at the Royal Farms Arena. Because they were so close to home, they'd decided to take a break from the tour bus to sleep in a house that didn't move. Pat was delighted by their decision. Most of his children and grandchildren lived in Baltimore, which meant it was rare for him not to see them all at least once a day.

Ailis, however, lived on the bus with her parents, traveling the world. As such, it was special whenever Patrick got to steal some alone time with the sweet child. Teagan assured him that once Ailis hit school age, they'd put down some roots, but Patrick wondered if that plan was changing. Just tonight over dinner, Teagan had been telling Keira about some homeschooling program she'd been looking into.

"*Och*, you poor child. You just crawl in here with Pop Pop tonight. I'll keep the bad dreams away so you can sleep."

Ailis's tears evaporated as a grin covered her face. She climbed onto his tall bed and he tucked her beneath the covers. She was only four, and the spitting image of her mother. Patrick had to catch himself time and again before he called Ailis by Teagan's name.

And the resemblance between the mother and daughter didn't end with looks. Their personalities and dispositions were just as similar.

Ailis had inherited her mother's whimsical ways—often wearing brightly colored clothing. That fact was driven home to him as he looked down at her neon-rainbow footie pajamas.

She also had a quietness to her nature, uncomfortable whenever attention was thrown in her direction. Ailis was extremely bashful, and it had taken him the better part of yesterday to get her to say more than a few words to him.

Teagan had shed some of her shyness over the past few years—with the help of Sky and about a million and twelve adoring fans. He hoped Ailis would manage to do the same. She was such a bright, funny little thing when she finally started talking.

"How about a story?" Patrick asked.

Ailis nodded her head enthusiastically. He'd read her no less than six picture books just a couple of hours earlier when he'd put her in bed, but he didn't want to turn the lights on and go down the hall in search of her favorite Dr. Seuss story.

"I'm going to tell you a story about a woman whose name is Ailis."

Ailis's eyes widened. "Like me?"

Patrick nodded.

"Nobody has a name like me."

"Well, this woman did. She lived hundreds and hundreds of years ago in Kilkenny."

"Is that in Ireland? Where you're from?"

Patrick nodded, always so impressed with the young child's memory. "It certainly is. This Ailis was so beautiful she had to hide her face with a veil." Patrick lifted the sheet over Ailis's face. "Like this."

Ailis giggled as she pulled the sheet back down. "Why did she have to hide her face?"

"Because she was so beautiful, people would faint whenever they saw her." Patrick put his hand on his head and pretended to be dizzy. "In fact, you're so pretty…"

Ailis tugged the covers back over her face, laughing with delight. "There. Now you're safe," she said from beneath the sheet. But then, because she was a little minx, she pulled the covers down quickly, saying, "Boo!"

Patrick pretended to pass out, much to Ailis's delight. They continued to play peek-a-boo, Ailis hiding and then reemerging, causing him to faint. After a few minutes, she tired of the game.

"So she never got to show anyone her face?" she asked.

Patrick shook his head. "No. She didn't. And I think that's a shame."

"Why?"

"Because beauty should never be hidden." Patrick considered Ailis's shyness. He worried about the little girl, living on a bus, surrounded only by adults most days. Teagan remarked that Ailis came alive whenever she was around her cousins. That comment had stuck in the back of his mind and bothered him a bit. While Teagan had been happy that her daughter was so close to and fond of her cousins, Patrick worried about the fact the little girl wasn't alive the rest of the time. Teagan said she was an avid reader, tackling books that were well beyond her age range, and that Ailis could spend hours reading so quietly in a corner of the bus that they'd forget she was there. "I want you to promise me something, Ailis."

"Okay."

"Don't do what the other Ailis did."

Ailis frowned, clearly confused.

He hastened to explain. "Don't hide yourself away. You're too beautiful—inside and out. I don't ever want you to be afraid to show people who you really are." Patrick grimaced. This lesson was going right over her head. She was too young to understand, and he was forcing the issue because his time with her was always so short. Even this visit was nearly over. Teagan, Sky and Ailis would be boarding the bus again tomorrow, despite the fact they'd only arrived yesterday, and it would be months before he'd see her again.

"I won't," she said so solemnly, Patrick wondered if he'd been mistaken about her understanding.

"I know you get shy around strangers."

Her brow creased. "Mommy tells me not to talk to them."

Yeah, he was messing this up. Teagan never let Ailis out of her sight, for good reason. They were always in different cities, surrounded by people they didn't know. Teagan's overprotectiveness had manifested itself in Ailis, which meant the child was constantly clinging to her mother's leg, hiding her face whenever anyone talked to her. She was particularly uncomfortable with the paparazzi and the cameras constantly flashing in her face.

While that was not a bad thing, he hated to think of any of his grandchildren cowering from life, dimming the lights that shone so brightly from them.

How many times had he wished Sunday had lived to see this incredible family they'd made?

"Your mommy is right. You shouldn't talk to strangers, but, Ailis, you shouldn't be afraid to talk to people that you know."

"They're all grownups," she said, by way of explanation.

"Doesn't matter. I want you to stop hiding behind your mom and start talking to people more. This beautiful mind," he touched her head, "and this beautiful heart," he touched her chest, "are too special to hide."

"Okay. I can talk to Mr. Les. He's nice."

Les Fossie was Sky's manager. And he was indeed a very nice man. "He'd be a fine one to talk to."

"And there's Bobby and Roxanne and Oliver."

He grinned as she named the members of Sky's band. "Maybe they can teach you how to play an instrument."

Ailis crinkled her nose and shook her head. "I don't want to do that."

Her quick response caught him off guard, especially considering both her parents were talented musicians. "Why not?"

"Because I want to live here one day, so I can play with Caitie and Lochlan and Paddy and Colm all the time, and you can't do that if you're in a band."

Of course, for Ailis, music was synonymous with travel and buses and a life lived in constant motion. "I see."

"When I'm bigger, I'm gonna come live here with you, Pop Pop."

Patrick tapped her on the tip of her nose. "I would like that very much." And then, because he worried, he asked, "Don't you like life on the bus?"

Her eyes widened with excitement. "Yeah. We went to this one place where they had a real Thomas the Tank Engine train and we got to ride in it, and then in this other place we got to go in an egg up to the top of this McDonald's M thing and look down. And then…" Ailis continued listing all the wondrous things she'd seen in her journeys, and Pat calmed down. She was an inquisitive, lively child who was doing just fine where she was.

Finally, after several minutes, Ailis yawned.

"But for now, I think we better try to sleep. If we're awake when your mommy gets home, we'll both be in trouble."

Ailis giggled. "She can't yell at you. You're *her* daddy."

Patrick made a horrified face. "You don't know your mommy."

Ailis settled beneath the covers and within seconds, she was asleep.

Oh, to have that ability, Patrick thought. The older he got, the harder sleep was to come by. Unless, of course, it was in the middle of the afternoon and he was in his recliner. That was probably his problem now. His ninety-minute nap earlier.

He lay in bed and thought about the sweet little girl sound asleep next to him. He sent up a brief prayer of thanks that he was still here and able to watch these little ones, his beloved grandchildren, grow up. He'd been blessed with his children and then again, with his grandchildren. He didn't take one second of his time with them for granted.

Then, as he always did, he sent up a special prayer to their guardian angel.

"Watch over this one, Sunday," he whispered. "She has so much more to offer than she knows."

Chapter One

Ailis sat on the couch and stared at the wall in front of her. She had no idea how much time had passed since she'd gotten home, found the letter and assumed this zombie-like pose. Minutes? Hours? Days?

Her gaze dropped slightly, catching sight of the letter on the coffee table. She closed her eyes rapidly before any of the words formed in her brain. When she opened them again, she made certain she was looking up. At the wall. Only the wall. The wall was safe.

Part of her was waiting for tears. That was the natural response, the one most women would have succumbed to.

She'd just been dumped. Big time. In a horrible fucking letter.

However, instead of crying her heart out, screaming curses into the empty room, beating her fists against the couch cushions, all she could manage was this numb silence.

Typical. Even alone with her broken heart, she couldn't find a way to express the pain with any semblance of noise or passion.

No wonder Paul had left.

The thought of his name worked. Triggered an emotion. Though it wasn't sadness. It was resignation.

She was an intelligent woman. If she looked back on the last six years reasonably, with a detached eye, she would have seen that they were a mismatch. It was obvious now.

Paul was driven, a climber. He was never going to be happy until he'd achieved every single goal he had set for himself. She knew that because she'd been there as he'd knocked a few off his list. He'd graduated top of his class at University of Maryland, where they'd met. He'd been accepted to Johns Hopkins School of Medicine. Then he'd gotten his residency at Hopkins, his dream job.

Ailis had been there beside him, either as a friend or a girlfriend, for nearly every part of that. She had been the perfect match for him during the college years because she'd enjoyed learning, and even though she wasn't studying medicine, she'd helped Paul with his coursework. She was a stronger student, something Paul took advantage of as she basically co-wrote all his papers and helped him memorize countless facts about the body and diseases. The two of them joked that she had a medical degree without the diploma.

He craved attention, the limelight. When he was in the room, his sheer dominant presence ensured that all eyes were on him as he discussed politics or offered medical advice or told some funny story about the antics of the doctors at the hospital. He'd been president of every club he had ever joined.

And she'd been lingering in the background like some creepy shadow. He'd referred to her as his silent rock on more than one occasion. Like a stupid fool, she had considered that a compliment, thinking he needed her somehow.

Probably because the political and social views he espoused were the ones she'd discussed with him. She was the one watching the news, reading the papers, forming opinions. They'd talk at length about countless topics when they were alone at night. Then, in social settings, he'd use her lines, her comments, professing them as his own, and his equally shallow friends would be totally impressed by his insight.

Before tonight, she'd actually bragged about how lucky she was to find a man whose personal beliefs aligned so closely to hers.

Now, the blinders were off. And she didn't like what she saw. She'd been a doormat.

Six years they'd been together. Eight, if she counted the two years prior to dating when they had simply been friends, hanging out in similar circles.

With Rhonda.

That name fired its own shots in her brain, evoked a different but just as powerful emotion. Rhonda had been her best friend since their freshman year of college when they'd been placed together as roommates in the dorm. That friendship had persevered and continued as they'd shared the same major and then, after graduation, been hired at the same marketing firm.

Rhonda was everything Ailis was not. Vivacious, lively, pretty. The life of every party. The fun one. She had been a solid C student, but she had the personality to overcome what she lacked in intelligence. How many times had she listened to friends and colleagues tease the two of them about opposites attracting? As loud and bubbly as Rhonda was, Ailis was the polar opposite. Quiet, introspective, calm.

People thought she was shy, but Ailis had never considered herself timid. In truth, she just didn't feel the need to be the center of attention. She was perfectly capable of carrying on conversations one-on-one with strangers and business clients. But in larger social settings, she preferred to find a quiet corner to observe and analyze. People-watching was one of her favorite things to do. She always felt like she learned more about people by watching them than she did by talking to them.

Obviously, she'd been watching the wrong people. Or, perhaps, she'd been observing the right people, but interpreting what she'd seen incorrectly.

Because Paul hadn't just left her. He'd left her for Rhonda.

Somewhere over the past few years, her boyfriend had fallen for her best friend. And she'd missed the signs. Completely.

That thought sent her gaze back to the letter. This time she forced herself to look at it. To let some of the words sink in.

You have no idea how difficult it is for me to write this letter to you, Ailis.

Yeah. Well. He should try it from her perspective. Because she was pretty sure reading it was way harder.

She glanced away again, taking in the living room of the apartment she shared with Paul. His departure had been deliberate, planned, well thought out. There were things missing. A lot of things. Though she hadn't looked, she was willing to bet she would discover his dresser drawers and his half of the closet empty, his toiletries gone.

He'd been a very busy boy today while she was at work. Paul had quickly and efficiently erased himself from her life. In less than ten hours.

She resumed her study of the wall in front of her, too tired to think about this right now. Maybe she'd pull that bottle of wine out of the fridge and drink her way into oblivion. She could figure out the rest of her life tomorrow.

Unfortunately, standing up and walking to the kitchen required more energy than she could muster.

Then the silence was interrupted viciously by a loud banging on the front door. Ailis jerked at the unexpected sound, her heart racing at the sudden noise. "Shit," she muttered, placing her trembling hand on her chest.

"Open the fucking door, Paul! Come out here, you goddamn prick!"

Ailis leaned back against the couch with a long sigh. Her day sucked enough. Adding Hunter Maxwell to it was like tossing salt into a gaping wound.

She didn't move to answer the door. Maybe he'd think no one was home and go away.

"You have five seconds to open this door before I kick the motherfucker in, you son of a bitch!"

Ailis groaned as she rose. She didn't doubt for a second he'd do exactly as he threatened. Which meant she'd be trying to figure out how to repair a doorframe at—she glanced at the clock—nine o'clock at night.

She'd been on the couch for three hours.

She unlocked the door and opened it, only just managing to step out of the path of the raging bull who didn't wait for an invitation to come in.

"He's not here," she said simply, hoping that would be enough to send Hunter packing.

Hunter stormed down the hallway, looking in every room, muttering every foul name in the book, and a few she'd never heard.

Finally, satisfied Paul wasn't there, he returned to the living room and, for the first time, he looked at her.

"What the fuck?!" His tone was complete bewilderment, mingled with absolute fury.

She shrugged, uncertain how to reply. It occurred to her, Hunter was actually the only other person on the planet who understood exactly how she felt at the moment. Because he'd been blindsided and taken down too.

That struck her as slightly funny in its irony. Primarily because she and Hunter had absolutely nothing else in common.

He reached into his jacket pocket and held out an envelope. "I found this when I got home."

Ailis recognized Rhonda's handwriting. Hunter had gotten a letter too. Been dumped exactly the same way she had.

He opened the envelope and pulled out an engagement ring. The one he'd given Rhonda only a few weeks ago, over the holidays. The one Rhonda had accepted with an excited squeal at their Friendsgiving celebration, everyone present, everyone thrilled as they offered their congratulations.

At the time, Ailis had been jealous of Rhonda, silently hoping that Paul took a page from Hunter's book, surprising her with a ring at Christmas.

He hadn't. Instead, he'd given her a cashmere sweater and a first-edition book of poetry she mentioned liking. Oh, and a freaking Starbucks gift card. As though he were her uncle rather than her boyfriend.

Ailis gestured toward the coffee table. "I got a letter too."

She hadn't intended her words as an invitation, but Hunter took them as such. He walked over, grabbed her letter and sank down into a chair to read it.

Part of her wanted to snatch it from his hands. It was personal, her own private hell.

But she understood as he read the words, his hands fisting the paper so tightly she thought it would tear, it wasn't just her pain.

She and Rhonda had been tight since college, but Paul and Hunter had been the best of friends since elementary school. They'd grown up as neighbors and they were closer than brothers. She'd always wondered how that friendship had stuck whenever she studied the two of them together. Hunter was faded jeans, hoodies and a scruffy beard, a hippie with shaggy auburn hair and pale blue eyes, while Paul was starched collars and clean-shaven, preppy, the classical tall, dark and handsome. Hunter was takeout and horror movies. Paul was fancy restaurants and the theater. Yet somehow, for the past twenty-plus years, they'd found a common ground—their love of the same sports teams—that kept them connected. That and a shared history.

"What the fuck?" he muttered again as he put her letter back on the coffee table. He bent his head, his elbows resting on his knees.

Ailis walked over and resumed her spot on the couch. She wasn't sure what to say. She and Hunter weren't friends. It was closer to say they merely tolerated each other's existence because they had to.

Hunter was the equivalent of a twenty-seven-year-old frat boy, despite the fact he'd never gone to college. He claimed high school had been more than enough for him. He partied too hard, laughed too loud, cussed like a sailor, and constantly teased her about being so quiet, calling her mouse, a nickname that annoyed her to no end. His idea of reading was flipping through magazines to look at the pictures. On more than one occasion, he'd seen her with a nose in a book and wondered aloud how she could waste so much time on something so boring. In his estimation, if a book was any good at all, they'd make it into a movie and he'd just watch that instead.

They had nothing in common except Paul and Rhonda.

And now, their broken hearts.

"You didn't see it coming?" she asked, probably because that was what was bugging her the most. She considered herself astute. The idea that Paul had hidden his true feelings for Rhonda from her so well was driving her insane.

He shook his head. "No. I thought she was happy." He looked up, his eyes dark with rage. "I'm going to fucking kill him."

While she was stuck in this weird state of numb devastation, Hunter's reaction was completely different, of course. He was in a murderous rage, and for the first time since reading Paul's letter, she was glad to know her former boyfriend was out of the state at the moment. It was probably the only thing saving his life.

Not that she took any pleasure in knowing he and Rhonda had gone full-on cliché and run away to Vegas together.

She'd been annoyed when Rhonda had called in sick today, knowing they were expected to give a very important presentation to potential clients at ten. Ailis had been stuck doing the whole thing on her own, which was nerve-racking as hell. Typically, Rhonda did the talking. Somehow she'd managed to get through it and they won the account.

They.

Fuck.

There was no way she could continue working with Rhonda. Some of Hunter's anger started to awaken in her.

"Fine. Kill him. I'm going to take care of the faithless, lying, bleach blonde bitch." The viciousness of her words, the heat behind them, sounded completely foreign even to her.

And apparently to Hunter too. She didn't lose her temper very often. His eyes widened, then approval set in. "I'll be your alibi if you'll be mine."

She grinned. "Deal."

For a second, they were able to smile, but the reprieve was brief when Hunter's eyes returned to her letter. It had been Paul's idea to set Rhonda and Hunter up on a blind date three years earlier. Ailis had predicted it would be a mistake, thinking them too much alike to get along. She'd been proven wrong.

Until now.

"I don't get it. She said yes. She was excited about the engagement. Why? Why would they do this?"

Ailis shrugged. Paul had never proposed to her, but that didn't mean they hadn't discussed the future. They'd made plans, dreamed of a big wedding and buying a house, having kids, saving for retirement. She hadn't built up those expectations out of thin air. They'd been real...at least to her.

"I don't know why." She didn't. She'd been sitting here for three hours, trying to wade through it all, searching for something that made sense. Nothing did.

"What am I supposed to do now?" His voice was laced with the pain she was searching for, trying to feel. Now that she thought about it, maybe she was in shock.

He slouched back in the chair and sighed heavily. "What now?" he repeated, more to himself than her.

It was a fair question. One she was sorry he didn't have an answer for. That meant she couldn't follow his lead. "I guess we...just...move on."

He looked at her as if she'd sprouted a second head. "Just like that? You're not going to fight for him?"

Fighting for him had never occurred to her. Not once. "No."

"So you're giving up?" He rolled his eyes and the same mockery he usually reserved for her returned. "Typical mouse move. Not sure why I'm surprised."

She narrowed her eyes, her anger finally blooming full force, finding a much more convenient recipient. "I'm not giving up. I'm just not settling."

"Settling?"

"Why would I beg someone to come back who doesn't want me? Why would I want someone so cruel, so *cowardly*, that he had to break up with me in a letter? He's an immature child, a selfish asshole, somebody who doesn't deem me worthy of any respect, any kindness or compassion. He couldn't stick around and face me. After six years, Hunter, I think I deserved a lot better than this."

Hunter stared at her, speechless for several moments. She was fairly certain that was the most she'd ever said to him, and it was obvious he hadn't realized she had a voice. Then he sat up in the chair. His posture didn't look nearly as defeated as it had a few minutes earlier.

"You're right. Fuck 'em."

That wasn't what she'd said. Exactly. Though it did sum it up pretty nicely.

"I'm not a mouse, Hunter. I'm just..." Her words faded. She didn't have a clue what she was anymore. For so many years, she'd been defined by her relationship with Paul. Paul's study partner, his girlfriend, his better half. His silent fucking rock.

Hunter was still studying her, and it felt as if it was the first time he'd ever really seen her. They'd been in each other's lives for years and their first impressions had stuck. She had put him in the man-child box. He'd put her in the mouse box. Neither of them had ever bothered to look beyond that.

"You're not crying," he said at last. "Most chicks would be bawling their eyes out right now. Instead, you're sitting here being all logical and shit."

While he didn't say it, she went ahead and finished his opinion in her head. The part about her not being normal. Ailis was used to feeling like the odd guy out. She definitely lacked the passion, the stubbornness, the heart-on-her-sleeve emotions that ran through the rest of her family so strongly. Hunter would have made a better Collins, now that she considered it.

She had always attributed her calm, quiet nature to the fact she hadn't grown up around her rambunctious cousins, or aunts and uncles, or Pop Pop. Her time with them as a child had been limited to occasional visits. And even though she'd moved back to Baltimore after college, she still didn't see them as much as she could have. She'd remained apart, always too busy with work or Paul.

She'd never felt that distance until now.

Now, she missed them, wanted to be surrounded by their craziness, their loud voices all talking at once and their unconditional love.

She wanted to be a part of that...to go home. Home to a place she'd never lived.

"I'm moving out of this apartment."

Hunter frowned, confused by her random pronouncement. "Okay. Where are you going to go?"

She smiled and used the phrase coined by her aunt Riley. "The Collins Dorm."

"I have no idea what that is."

"The apartment over my family's Irish pub. A lot of my cousins live there now."

"Cool. I'm keeping my place. Rhonda obviously isn't planning to come back. She packed up all her shit."

"Sounds good."

"What about your job? You and Rhonda work together."

She'd avoided thinking about that, but there was no denying she couldn't return to the marketing firm. In truth, the job had never felt like the right fit for her anyway. Just another place where she was a square peg trying to fit into a round hole. "I'm going to quit."

"Damn. That's pretty rash, don't you think?"

She shook her head. "No. I can't work in the same building as...her."

"I get that."

"I'm pretty sure I can get a job waiting tables at the pub until I find something else."

"I guess I'm lucky. There's no danger of me running into either of them at the hotel." Hunter helped run a local inn with his aunt and uncle. His parents had died in a car crash when he was a teenager, and his great-aunt and uncle, older and childless, had taken him in, loved him as their own.

"Baltimore is a big enough city that we can probably avoid them forever." She knew that was a pipe dream, but right now, the idea of seeing Paul and Rhonda together was too painful to think about.

"I might start my band back up. Rhonda made me drop it. Said she hated how much it took me away from her. I was stupid to give up on it. I really miss playing my guitar in front of a crowd."

"I forgot about your band." Paul had dragged Ailis to more than a handful of Hunter's performances when they'd first started dating. He wasn't bad. Actually, he was very good. The rest of the musicians performing with him, however, had been mediocre at best.

He gave her a sad grin. "Yeah. Sounds stupid, but I always used to dream I'd make it big in music. Write some Grammy-winning song and travel the world performing." He winked as he added, "Sleep with a different groupie every night."

"I lived that life. It's not as awesome as it sounds."

"Really? Never pegged you as the groupie type."

She rolled her eyes, hung up on the idea that Hunter actually wrote music. That tidbit surprised her. "I grew up on the road. You know, it's not all glitz and glamour."

"Some of it must be cool."

21

She nodded, recalling that there was actually a lot about it that was terrific. She'd pushed memories of those parts away, mainly because of Paul's disdain for the musician's lifestyle. He'd turned his nose up the few times they'd been on her parents' bus, claiming he'd go mad in such a small space. For some stupid reason, she would back up his assertions rather than fight them.

"Yeah," she admitted. "Some of it is really fun."

"Sometimes I forget who your parents are. You never talk about them much."

Ailis didn't bother to point out that this was, hands down, the longest conversation she'd ever had with Hunter. But he was right. She didn't discuss her famous parents very often. Not because she wasn't incredibly proud of them. Truth was she adored her mom and dad, and there were very few days that went by where she didn't see or speak to one of them on the phone.

However, she had learned at a very young age that some of the friendships she thought she'd made weren't built on anything more than kids wanting to get close to her so they'd have access to rock stars. Her silence in regards to her parents was based on self-preservation. It allowed her to not have to wonder if people liked her for her, and not Sky Mitchell and Teagan Collins. She had been friends with Paul nearly a year before he figured out who her folks were. It helped that her folks had elected to give her and her sister, Fiona, her dad's real last name, instead of Mitchell.

"Yeah," Hunter said, more to himself than her. "I'm going back to music."

It was a weird conversation, but for some strange reason, Ailis felt almost comforted by it. She'd come up with a plan and she'd talked it out with someone. Why that suddenly made everything seem more bearable was a mystery. But it did.

"We're going to be okay."

Hunter looked at her as if he wanted to believe her, but couldn't quite grasp it yet. "I guess we're not the first people on the planet to get the shit kicked out of us. And we won't be the last."

"No. We're not. What are you going to do tonight?"

He shrugged. "Go home, fall into a bottle of bourbon, feel sorry for myself, probably send Rhonda a hundred texts I'll regret in the morning."

Ailis giggled. God, she really must be teetering on the edge of insanity if anything coming out of Hunter's mouth amused her. "Give me your phone."

Hunter handed his cell over without question or complaint. Ailis put her number in under Rhonda's name as he watched, his grin growing.

"Drink enough bourbon and you'll forget about that switch. This way, the texts will come to me and you won't have to regret anything tomorrow. I'll delete them without reading them. Promise."

"I'd appreciate that. What about you? You want my number in Paul's place?"

She shook her head. "No. That's not going to be a problem. You know me. I'm going the silent-treatment route."

"I think you should text him. Tell him off. Not good to keep all that bottled up."

"Maybe I will," she lied, knowing she'd never do it. She avoided confrontation like the plague.

"You going to be alright?"

She nodded slowly. "Yeah. I'm going to crawl into bed and have a good long cry. Then tomorrow, I'll pack up my stuff, move home and cry on my cousins' shoulders. And at some point, I'll stop crying."

"Very logical of you." Hunter stood up and she followed suit, walking behind him as he headed toward the door. He opened it, and then turned to face her. "Thanks, Ailis."

It was the first time he'd ever called her by her real name instead of mouse. And she didn't care for the formality of it. Too much had already changed tonight. She wanted to hold on to just one thing. Even if it was something stupid and annoying.

"Mouse," she corrected.

He chuckled. "You're the fiercest mouse I've ever met. And I think you might have saved me tonight."

She sniffled as the first of the tears decided to make their appearance, his kindness doing her in. "No problem," she said, hating the thickness of her voice. He'd helped her too. More than he'd ever know.

"Take care of yourself, mouse."

"You too," she whispered, even though he'd already left. She closed the door, locked it and gave up the fight, letting the tears fall.

Chapter Two

Ten months later…

Ailis walked into Pat's Pub, stopping just over the threshold to turn and look at her date for the evening.

"I had a nice time." That was lie number one.

"So did I," he assured her. "Maybe we could do it again sometime."

"I'd like that." Lie number two.

"I'll give you a call."

"I look forward to it." And there was whopper number three. Mentally, she tried to decide if she should make a trip to the cell phone store tomorrow to get a new number. Ray struck her as the type of guy who would call twenty times a day for the next year and a half, no matter how many times she sent him to voicemail. Which would be every time.

She smiled as she held out her hand. A handshake was the most he was getting. If he leaned in and tried to steal a kiss, he wouldn't even get the handshake.

Ray took the hint and shook her hand. "I'll talk to you soon."

She nodded, forcing a smile, unable to utter another lie. Her karma was already on shaky ground.

Ray left and she gave her cousin, Padraig, a half-hearted wave. He was manning the bar tonight. Ordinarily, she'd stop for a chat, but tonight she just didn't have it in her. She started toward the staircase at the back of the pub that would lead to the Collins Dorm and her bedroom. She was done with tonight.

Ugh. She was done with her life. Something had to give.

Luckily, the regulars seemed to figure out she was in no mood to talk by her quick nods and hasty retreat.

She'd just reached the door to the stairway when she heard her name.

Not being called out—but sung.

Ailis turned toward the stage just as Hunter sang, "Ailis, don't leave so soon. I need you to, report to the stage," to the tune of "Hey Jude." None of the patrons seemed to mind the fact Hunter was screwing up their favorite Beatles song. Instead, they chuckled and pointed her toward the stage as if she had no choice.

"Hunter wants to talk to you, honey," Mrs. Warren said.

Ailis sighed. She should have known an easy escape wouldn't be possible. She looked at Hunter, shook her head wearily and pointed to the floor above their heads, hoping he'd get the message. Of course, the ornery man didn't acknowledge her unspoken request. Instead, he just kept rewriting one of John and Paul's greatest hits.

"This is my last song. Don't make me come up and get you," he sang, taking some liberties with the notes as "get" was dragged out over at least four or five of them.

Ailis gave up. There were too many people looking at her now, and she wanted him to stop singing to her and finish the song right. She hated being the center of attention, and Hunter knew it.

She crossed her arms and leaned against the back wall. Hunter gave her a devilish grin, pleased to have won. He returned to the classic lyrics as several patrons joined in. And then, at last, the song—and his set—was over.

She walked to the stage as he unplugged the amp, put his guitar away, and packed up several cords.

"Given the fact you're home before midnight, I'm going to go out on a limb and say the date sucked," he said before she could chastise him for his song.

"It was lousy."

"What happened?"

"What happened is you and I both squandered our twenties dating the wrong people and now all the decent men and women are married. What's left on the market isn't a pretty sight."

Hunter chuckled. "I wouldn't say that. I've gone out with more than a few—"

"Sleeping with is not the same as going out with, Hunter. We've gone over this before."

"Maybe not, but sex helps take the edge off. You should try it sometime. You're wound up tighter than a drum."

She sat on the edge of the stage and looked across the pub as she spoke. "You know I'm not going to do that."

Hunter dropped down next to her. "I'm being serious, Ailis. You've only slept with one guy your entire life and it was fucking stick-in-the-mud Paul Marshall. Which means you probably didn't do anything more exciting than missionary."

"You know, he used to be your best friend."

"That's right, he was. I know the man and all his faults. That's how I know your sex life was uneventful. Go out and get laid. Extra credit if you do something kinky."

They'd had this argument too many times in the past year, which meant she knew exactly how it was going to end. At an impasse. With her bemoaning his man-slut ways and him calling her a virgin. Neither of them made those comments with any heat or meanness. It was just the way it was between her and Hunter. They teased constantly, but everything they said was out of fondness, out of friendship.

"I'm not sleeping with anyone I'm not in love with." Ailis had always intended to be like her mother, who had been a virgin when she'd met and fell in love with Sky Mitchell, rock superstar. Ailis loved the romance of that and wanted to be the same. Devoted to the love of her life.

Then Ailis had given her virginity to the man she'd thought she was going to marry.

Six years of her life dedicated to Paul. And then he'd dumped her for Rhonda, leaving her in Baltimore with an equally jilted Hunter.

Ailis hadn't expected to see Hunter again after he'd left her apartment that terrible night ten months earlier. She believed they'd both move on and their paths wouldn't cross again.

Then he had appeared in the pub a month later. He'd ordered a beer. And then another. And then her shift ended and she'd joined him. They talked like old friends, war buddies, and they hadn't stopped talking since.

"Dear God. I have no idea why love and sex are connected in your mind. Completely different creatures if you ask me."

She was used to hearing that line too. "There's nothing abnormal with wanting to fall in love and get married, Hunter."

"What's wrong with being single? I love my life these days. Kicking my own ass for hanging on to Rhonda for as long as I did."

Hunter had sworn off long-term relationships after Rhonda left, and he'd decided bachelorhood was the life for him. Ailis suspected his bold proclamation was only fifty-percent truth. The other fifty was the part that wasn't about to get hurt again, even if it did mean he had to die a lonely old man.

"I don't want to be single. I want a house and kids."

He sighed. He wanted the exact opposite. Hunter's future plans included what Ailis had lived in her past. A tour bus. A different city every night. Paparazzi dogging his every step. Fame. Fortune.

And if Hunter got his wish, a million big-boobed, blonde groupies ready to act out every depraved sex act in the man's repertoire night after night.

"You're wasted in this pub, mouse."

That was the one part of this argument she couldn't win. Because he was right. She'd come home after the breakup to lick her wounds. She'd resigned her position at the firm with the intention of finding another job in marketing, but she hadn't done that. Mainly because, when she'd majored in marketing in college, working in an office cubicle had never been her intention.

She had actually planned to take an internship with Les, her parents' band manager. Then the marketing firm job offer had come right around the same time Paul got his residency at Hopkins. At the time, it had made sense for her to stay in Baltimore with him, to work on building a life with him here, one that didn't involve a lot of travel.

Now, of course, she was completely adrift, jobless. She'd stuck with waitressing in the pub, burrowing in to soak up every bit of safety and security her family provided.

"I know," she admitted. He wasn't the only person to point it out to her. She heard it constantly. From him, her parents, her cousins. Even Pop Pop had pulled her aside a couple of weeks ago to ask her what her future career plans were. "I'm feeling very lost these days."

"It's just going to take us some time to get our sea legs back."

She appreciated that he got where she was coming from, that he was riding this same emotional wave. Good days. Bad days. Just last month, she'd gotten one of his drunk, rambling, how-could-you-do-this-to-me texts to Rhonda. She had told Hunter she wouldn't read them, but she hadn't carried through with that promise. Mainly because hearing him speak the words she felt, the ones she couldn't say to Paul, helped her, made her feel less lonely and fucked up.

"Come on," Hunter said, standing, and then reaching down to pull her up as well. "Go upstairs and grab some cousins. We're going out."

She shook her head, but he waved his hand to cut off her complaint.

"We're getting shitfaced, A. Drinking tequila, chasing it with Natty Boh and dancing our asses off."

She crinkled her nose at his mention of National Bohemian beer. "I'll drink the tequila, but you're on your own with the beer."

He laughed as he pointed to his instrument and amp. "I'll load this stuff in the car while you rally the troops."

As she climbed the stairs to her apartment, she tried to figure out how she'd been roped into a night out so easily. It was Hunter's fault. Experience had proven it was easier to just go along with him. Resistance was futile.

"Hey, Ailis. How was your date?" Sunnie asked as soon as she entered the living room.

"It sucked. Hunter and I are heading downtown to go clubbing. Who's in?" Ailis asked, completely unsurprised when Sunnie and Finn bounced up instantly. They both had their mother Riley's love of adventure. There were very few parties the two of them willingly missed, and typically their only reason for saying no was illness or a hangover from the previous night's party.

Colm shook his head, looking far too comfortable in the recliner with a beer in hand. "Long day at work. Count me out."

"Where's Caitlyn?" Ailis asked.

Colm chuckled. "Did happy hour at her folks' house with her mom. Sounds like she and Aunt Keira went in for a second bottle of wine, giggling their heads off when she called earlier. She's crashing there tonight."

Her oldest cousin, Caitlyn had moved back home about the same time as Ailis after suffering a painful breakup with her own cheating ex, Sammy. It was a freaking epidemic. And while Ailis would never wish unhappiness on any of her cousins, having Caitlyn move in to share a room with her had helped so much. Between her cousin and Hunter, Ailis hadn't felt nearly as alone in her sadness.

Ailis blew out an exasperated breath as she recalled their Friendsgiving celebration last week. It had been a far cry from the previous year, when she and Hunter had spent the same type of celebration with Paul and Rhonda and a much different crowd. Paul's friends were typically residents at the hospital who were only capable of discussing work, and Rhonda had included half a dozen people from their marketing firm, whom Ailis didn't consider friends as much as colleagues. As such, the celebration—with the exception of Hunter's proposal—had been fairly boring.

It felt as if she'd gotten it right this year. She'd spent it right here with her cousins, Hunter and a few other close friends. She and Hunter had made a pact that they would be grateful for their blessings, stop focusing on the negative, and turn things around. He was going to stop spinning his wheels as far as his music career was concerned, and she was going to find a real job and date more often.

One week in and she hadn't even bothered to open her resume on the computer to clean it up. And all she had found was Ray, the most boring man on the planet.

"Padraig and Yvonne are working until close, so it looks like it's just us," Sunnie said as she rushed down the hallway toward her bedroom. "Let me change into something more hootchie and call Leo. Maybe he'll want to meet us downtown."

Ailis sank down on the couch to wait for her with Finn and Colm. They discussed the cold weather, what to buy Pop Pop for Christmas, and which club would be the best to hit. Hunter arrived upstairs at the same time Sunnie returned to the living room.

"You all ready?" Hunter asked.

Sunnie nodded. "I told Leo I'd text him once we decided where we're going."

"Cool," Hunter said. "I'll leave my car here and we can cab it." Hunter had his phone out, the app open and the ride requested before they hit the bottom of the stairs.

The trip to the club was fun and by the time they arrived, Ailis was laughing. Something she hadn't anticipated after shaking Ray's hand at the front door of the pub. Leave it to Hunter and her cousins to know how to cheer her up.

Hunter had actually been doing that a lot lately. Initially, in those early months, they'd kept each other going, a regular two-man band of brothers. They'd been in the trenches together, suffered the same pain. When she was down, he was there, picking her up. And when he had a rough night, she did the same for him. Those nights were growing fewer and farther between these days.

The music was thumping loudly when they arrived. Sunnie's friend Leo was waiting for them at the door, and the five of them fought their way through the crowd in search of a table. Mercifully they found one near the back where the music wasn't quite as deafening. The waitress took their orders—a round of tequila shots and five Coronas—and they settled in to watch the dancing.

At least, she and Hunter did. It was a physical impossibility for Sunnie to hear music and not move.

"Let's dance!" she begged.

Hunter shook his head. "You go ahead. We'll wait for the drinks. Meet you out there later."

Sunnie dragged her brother and Leo out onto the floor, while Ailis looked around.

"I think Baltimore is getting smaller," she said after a quick survey of the bar.

"What do you mean?"

"I used to be able to go out and not know anyone. I swear to God nowadays it's the same people every weekend."

Hunter leaned closer. "I think they all just look the same."

"No." She shook her head. "I'm telling you. We're trapped in a single-person's vortex. This is seventh-level-of-hell kind of stuff."

"It was one bad date, Ailis."

"I wish it had been. But the truth is it's been four bad dates in six months."

Hunter grinned. "You counted?"

"Of course I did. Besides, it's not like four is that high a number."

"I didn't count."

She rolled her eyes. "Probably because you can't count that high."

"Smart-ass." Hunter ruffled her hair as she tried to beat his hand away with a giggle.

"I thought that was you two," a male voice said.

Ailis and Hunter looked up at the same time and found themselves face-to-face with the exes.

They'd managed to avoid this for almost an entire year. Somehow, Ailis had let that fact lure her into a false sense of security. While it wasn't unusual to hear news about Paul or Rhonda on occasion from shared acquaintances, she hadn't had to face her foes until now.

Paul had texted her a few times after he'd first returned from Vegas with his new wife in tow, claiming he wanted the chance to explain his actions in person. She'd ignored every single one of them and eventually blocked his number. She told herself it was because she didn't feel generous enough to listen to his apology, to give him the opportunity to try to make amends. After all, the time for chatting was before he'd left town. Not after.

Rhonda, however, had remained a coward, never once contacting her...or Hunter. No matter how many times he got wasted and texted her. And by "her," Ailis meant *herself*.

So, in all fairness, Rhonda didn't know how desperately Hunter had wanted to see her, talk to her. But Ailis did, and her disdain for her former best friend grew with every brokenhearted text until she couldn't look at the woman as anything less than a complete fucking bitch.

"Paul," Ailis said in surprise. "Rhonda." She and Hunter had gone clubbing countless times and they'd never once run into Paul and Rhonda. She'd suspected that was why they kept doing it. Clubs were their safe zone.

"What are you guys doing here?" Hunter's tone was too chilly to be mistaken for anything other than anger. Time hadn't healed Hunter's wounds. The man could hold a grudge like nobody. Not that she was faring much better.

Of course, Paul had never proposed to Ailis, claiming he needed to get his medical career sorted before he considered making that leap.

Hunter *had* proposed. And Rhonda had said yes. Then she'd left the ring he'd given her and a note on the coffee table and run off to say "I do" to someone else. Well, not just anybody else. Hunter's best friend. So yeah, his anger was completely justified.

Rhonda stumbled a bit in the face of Hunter's hostility, and Ailis tried to recall what it was that had made the woman someone she'd considered such a great friend. She was always just a bit too much, when Ailis thought about it. Always trying too hard to be the center of attention, talking too loud, wearing clothes that were super sexy, makeup that was too heavy and flipping her long blonde hair in a flirty way meant to attract men. And on top of that, she sure as hell wasn't loyal or trustworthy. So why had Ailis hung out with her for so long? She could only assume it was the work thing and the similar circle of friends' thing.

Rhonda glanced at Paul uncomfortably. "Um. We haven't been out in ages. We've both been so busy with work. Everyone really misses you there, Ailis."

Ailis didn't reply. She merely nodded.

"We thought we'd take this last chance to get out and dance before..." Paul said.

"Before?" Ailis said, immediately kicking herself for taking his bait so easily.

"Rhonda is pregnant. Due in May. Probably the last time we're going to get to go out for a while."

Hunter remained stone-faced, silent, which was typically Ailis's job. She didn't have a clue how to respond to the bomb just dropped at their table, so she dug deep and threw out her biggest lie of the night. One word laced with so much insincerity it could sink a boat.

"Congratulations."

Paul didn't acknowledge her statement. He was looking too closely at her sitting next to Hunter. "I didn't realize the two of you were friends."

Ailis resisted the urge to finger comb the hair Hunter had just messed up. She tried to tell herself she didn't care what he thought, but she wasn't there yet. Especially not when Rhonda was standing there looking like a fashion model even though she was three months pregnant.

There was something about the way Paul looked at her, almost as if he pitied her, that hurt.

Then it pissed her off. After all, he was the bastard who'd stolen six years of her life then left her here— twenty-eight years old and club hopping, hoping to meet the *real* Mr. Right, since he'd turned out to be Mr. Wrong.

"Yeah, we're friends. We hang out," Ailis said, not sure how else to reply.

"But you two don't have anything in common. You don't even like each other," Paul said, still speaking to Ailis as if she were a child he needed to protect from her own inexperience and naivety.

"I wouldn't say that," Hunter answered, wrapping his arm around her and pulling her close.

Ailis was stunned when he followed that unexpected movement up with a kiss to her forehead that was definitely more than friendly.

"Are you two going out?" Rhonda asked, obviously as shocked as Ailis was at the moment.

Hunter was wasting himself with music. His true talents clearly lie in acting. He never bothered to look at Rhonda. Instead, he stared at Ailis as if she hung the moon. "Oh yeah. Finally opened my eyes and realized that this angel had been standing right in front of me all along."

She wanted to blame Hunter's sudden insanity on alcohol, but they hadn't gotten their drinks yet.

Then he went completely around the bend, leaning closer and kissing her. On the lips. It wasn't a brushing glance, either. It was a legit kiss, full of heat and—whoa—a whole bunch of other things she couldn't even begin to describe.

If Hunter was doing this as some sort of joke, he was falling way short.

Because the kiss didn't make her want to laugh. It made her want to take all her clothes off. Here. Now.

Hunter's tongue darted out to stroke her lower lip a split second before he pulled away. He cupped her cheek with one hand, the touch full of affection and fondness. It was melting her insides.

Hunter's eyes remained locked on hers even as he spoke to the other couple. "Sorry. I have a hard time resisting her."

"I...see," Paul said, his tone wooden, unreadable. Ailis couldn't tell if her ex was angry or skeptical or annoyed or just bored. "Well, I guess we should leave you two to your...date."

Mercifully, the waitress returned with their shots and beers—impeccable timing, since things had just gotten mega-awkward—and Paul took Rhonda's hand.

"Enjoy your drinks," Paul said coldly, the venom in his tone taking Ailis aback. What the hell did *he* have to be pissed about?

"It was, um, great to see you both again," Rhonda said, though it was obvious she didn't really think so.

Ailis forced a smile and a quick nod. Hunter merely shot daggers at the other couple with his eyes until they beat a hasty retreat.

"Sooooo," Ailis dragged out. "What the hell, man?"

Hunter pretended not to understand her question. "What?"

"Why would you tell them we're dating? We're not. And even if we don't see them anymore, we do still have friends in common. They're going to find out that was a lie."

Hunter was quiet for three heartbeats, his expression still dark. "I don't care. I didn't like the way that son of a bitch was looking at you."

So she hadn't imagined it. The pity in Paul's eyes, as if she was destined to live life as a spinster.

"You did that for me?"

"He's a fucking prick. Walking around with his Dr. God complex. Thinking he's the best thing that ever happened to you, convinced you can't find better. He's lucky I kissed you. My other option was punching his fucking lights out for being such an arrogant asshole."

Ailis was more touched than she'd ever been in her life. Unfortunately, that feeling was fleeting, replaced by a much more familiar one. The one she hadn't managed to kick since Paul had told her they weren't a "good fit" in his letter, as if she were a shoe that pinched. As always, that small part of her that she hated reared its head, making her doubt her worth. "You don't think he's—"

Hunter rolled his eyes. "I swear to God, if you ask if he's right, if you are seriously sitting here thinking that you're never going to find anyone else, I'm gonna have to kiss you again."

Typically, confidence wasn't an issue for her, but it had been a long, lonely not-quite year filled with really bad dates. While she tried to be optimistic about her chances for love, that hope was stretched paper thin.

Or it had been...until that kiss.

Then she considered pushing the point, not because she believed she was unlovable—but because she liked the idea of Hunter kissing her again. However, her voice was too flirty to pull it off. "I'm just saying I think maybe if you wanted to try—"

"Stop looking at me like that," he said, interrupting her mid-coy, which was good because she really sucked at flirting.

"Like what?"

"You know what I'm talking about, mouse. We can't kiss again."

It was on the tip of her tongue to ask why not, but she was afraid he'd have a really good reason, one that might convince her not to go for a few more of those bone-rattling, shake-her-to-the-core kisses.

Her expression must not have changed, because Hunter groaned and picked up a shot glass to hand to her. "Jesus. Here. Mother's milk. To cure all awkward situations."

She and Hunter tapped shot glasses and downed the tequila. "Or to make them more awkward," she joked, struggling hard to get them back on familiar ground.

They reached across the table at the same time, laughing as they helped themselves to Sunnie and Finn's shots. Her cousins were still out on the dance floor. They didn't need them.

"Or to get you so drunk you forget what I just did," Hunter clarified as they threw back the second shots.

She was never going to forget that kiss. Ever.

Hunter caught the waitress's eye and twirled his finger—the universal sign for another round—as they both eyeballed the last shot, the odd guy out.

"What makes you think you deserve that one?" he asked as she started to reach it.

"My night was worse than yours," Ailis said, laying out her case for why she deserved the last shot of tequila. "Ray spent at least forty-five minutes of the date talking about the latest episode of *Real Housewives of Atlanta*. Spoiler alert. Apparently, they're all catty bitches."

Hunter chuckled. "He really watches that show?"

"Yeah, and that discussion was disturbing enough until it turned to his antiquated opinions of marriage. Whole thing was completely horrifying. I win, right?"

Hunter never gave in easily. "I'd bring up the fact that I just came face-to-face with the woman who ripped my heart out as an argument, but you have that same ace in the hole. So that one's a draw."

"Which means I'm in the lead."

"And I still need to get you drunk enough to forget my brief moment of insanity. You know that kiss wouldn't have affected you so much if you'd listen to me and get laid occasionally."

"It wasn't *that* great a kiss," she fired back, the words *liar, liar, pants on fire* singsonging their way through her brain.

"Take the shot, mouse. Then we're going to dance."

"When did I stop yelling at you for calling me mouse?"

"You know when. And you can go ahead and admit to liking it now. I won't rub it in too bad."

She rolled her eyes, but didn't argue. In truth, she'd never had a nickname, and she didn't feel any insult from Hunter when he said it. Not since he'd called her a fierce mouse and looked at her like she was someone he respected. Maybe it had started as a way to tease her for her quietness, but now it felt like his friendly pet name for her. Something that had moved them away from merely being brokenhearted buddies and toward a genuine friendship.

The third shot went down easier than the first two, providing a relaxing heat that worked its way through every part of her. All the rough edges inside went fuzzy, soft, and something shook itself clear. "I'm going to stop dating for a little while."

"What? Where did that come from?"

"I jumped back into the fray too soon. My issues with Paul were less about us and more about me. I gave him way too much control. Sacrificed things that made me happy to ensure his. I gotta figure out who I am first before I try to make my life fit with someone else's."

Hunter nodded, giving her that look that she'd seen on his face a lot in the past year. He always seemed impressed by her, like she was a pleasant surprise he hadn't expected. Initially, the expression had annoyed her. Now it amused her.

"That's really smart, A. I'm going to do it with you. Focus completely on my music. To hell with dating and love and all that crap. Operation Solo Act has just begun."

Hunter took her hand, leading her to the dance floor, and for the next few hours, they moved in time with the heart-pounding beat, only breaking occasionally for more tequila and beer.

He'd told her they were getting shitfaced. He hadn't lied.

Finn was the one to call uncle and, for the first time in their lives, it fell to Sunnie and her brother to be the responsible ones. They called for the cab and poured Hunter and Ailis into it around three a.m.

Ailis convinced Hunter to spend the night on their couch, mainly because she wasn't sure she could stay awake through three stops—they'd dropped Leo off first—and she was on the verge of passing out.

They all stumbled upstairs to the apartment together. Hunter fell onto the couch without taking off his coat or shoes. Finn and Sunnie laughed at how quickly he went down before heading to their own rooms. Ailis dragged herself along the hallway wall, letting it hold her up as she made her way to her bedroom.

She touched her lips, recalling Hunter's kiss again. He hadn't kissed her because he wanted her.

He'd actually kissed her for a reason that felt better than being wanted. Unfortunately, she was too drunk to figure out why that was true.

She sat on the edge of her bed and the room swayed. That wasn't good. It took her several minutes to strip off her shoes, socks, coat and jeans. The rest was just going to have to stay. She was too tired to take anything else off.

Ailis had just put her head on the pillow when Hunter appeared.

"Scoot over," he urged.

"No." Ailis lifted a floppy arm and pointed across the room. "Sleep in Cait's bed."

He ignored her, physically pushing her to one side of the bed as he claimed the other. She was flimsy as a rag doll and unable to put up much resistance.

He lay down on his back and pulled her toward him, her cheek resting on his chest. He'd managed to lose his shoes and coat somewhere, but he was still fully dressed.

Because it was a twin bed, it was a tight fit. Regardless, he positioned them in such a way that it worked.

"I don't want to sleep by myself."

"I'm not having sex with you, Hunter."

He chuckled. "I'm not talking about sex. Swore it off, remember? Sometimes it's nice to just sleep with somebody."

She frowned, too drunk to be reasonable. Hunter always wanted sex. "Why don't you want to have sex with me?"

"Seriously?" he asked. "You're offended that I don't want what *you* don't want?"

Ailis lifted her head and looked at him, not bothering to repeat the question, even though it was one she'd thought about before. Hunter flirted with anything with boobs, constantly turning on the charm. With everyone but her. For her, it was…just buddies. Just pals.

Or so she'd thought. That kiss had confused things. It hadn't been friendly. Not in the slightest.

"Three reasons," he said, forging on, even though she hadn't said anything. "Number one, I drank way too much tequila and I'm pretty sure he," Hunter pointed at his cock, "isn't up for it. Number two, you just swore off guys so you can find yourself. And finally, even if you hadn't made that last vow, I'm not telling you I love you just so I can fuck you. I've never lied to you, A. Don't wanna start now."

"Oh. Yeah." She put her head back down on his chest. Those arguments made sense to her tequila-soaked brain. She'd vowed she wouldn't sleep with anyone she wasn't in love with. And Hunter knew her well enough by now to know she meant it...when she was sober.

The problem was that brought up another worry, one she hadn't been able to let go of since seeing Paul, despite the tequila eraser she'd employed. "Why doesn't anyone want to marry me?"

"You're backsliding."

"No, I'm not. Tomorrow I'll be strong again. Tonight, I just want to try to understand all the pieces."

"Seems like you'd be better off reaching for those answers when you're sober."

"I won't ask the questions then."

"You gotta start talking to people more, A. And I don't just mean me and your family. You've got a lot of smart stuff to say."

"You're avoiding my question."

Hunter sighed and wrapped the arm around her shoulders tighter, tucking her closer. With his free hand, he reached over and touched her face, before finding her earring. He fiddled with it in a way that was strangely arousing as he spoke.

"You just haven't met the right guy."

"I thought I had. And he picked Rhonda."

"Ailis," Hunter started, and she knew what he was going to say. She cut him off at the pass.

"I'm not still hung up on him. I swear. That's not what this is about. It's just...I can't figure out what the difference is. You would have married Rhonda, wouldn't you? If she and Paul hadn't run away, you would have..."

He sighed. "I would have married her. And it would have been a mistake."

They'd discussed the breakup countless times before, and they'd both come up with plenty of reasons why they'd been lucky with their near misses. She always wondered if the reasons were valid or just comforting. "What is it that makes guys want to marry her and not me?"

"She puts out on the first date," he teased.

"You're an asshole. All guys are assholes."

"Yep. It's about time you figured that out."

They laughed together for a few minutes and Ailis was just about to fall asleep when he spoke again.

"She's pregnant, Ailis."

Ailis had been trying to forget about that. "Yeah. I hope she retains a lot of water and her ankles swell."

Hunter chuckled. "Jesus, mouse. Is that as mean as you get? Swollen ankles?"

"I believe in karma."

"I guess we did okay tonight. Us against them."

She had noticed lately that Hunter no longer referred to their great heartbreaks as solo occurrences, but as a thing they shared. "Yeah. I guess."

"Sorry I dragged you out. I know you wanted to stay in. If you had, we wouldn't have—"

"I'm glad we ran into them," she murmured. "Now it's out of the way. Pressure's off. Besides, the rest of the night was a blast."

They were quiet again, and Ailis was convinced he'd finally passed out. She was wrong.

"We're a couple of sad cases," Hunter mumbled sleepily.

"Yeah. I guess we are."

"We gotta stick to our goals. Ten months is long enough to feel sorry for ourselves. From now on, Rhonda and Paul are the past. Hunter and Ailis are the future."

She grinned at his pep talk. The way he said it almost made it sound like they were a couple, rather than two friends determined to find themselves, to make their way on their own.

"Everything good is going to happen this year, Hunter. Everything."

"Everything," he muttered, his deep breathing letting her know he'd finally fallen asleep. In her bed. She considered moving over into Caitlyn's side of the room, but changed her mind. It had been a long time since she'd slept in a bed with someone.

He was right.

It was nice.

Chapter Three

Ailis looked across the table where Sunnie and Hunter were laughing over some card he'd laid down in their cutthroat game of Cards Against Humanity.

It was New Year's Eve. And she was still living in Collins Dorm. Still essentially jobless.

She'd been dumped almost a year ago, and apart from the two moves she'd made the day after receiving the letter—moving out and quitting her job—she hadn't made one single forward step since.

To make matters worse, Caitlyn was out celebrating this New Year on a yacht with a man she'd met just before the holidays. She'd started dating Lucas Whiting, supposedly under the guise of spying on the man. He wanted to buy Pat's Pub, something that would only happen when hell froze over. However, Ailis suspected Caitlyn's feelings for Lucas had changed lately.

Caitlyn was obviously going to spend the night with the billionaire, and Ailis was too drunk to bother to shield her jealousy, even though she adored her cousin.

Leave it to Caitlyn to find a guy when she wasn't even looking.

Meanwhile, Ailis couldn't even manage to find herself. And she was sitting right there in her own skin.

"Come on, guys," Colm called from his spot on the couch, turning the channel to *New Year's Rockin' Eve*. "Take a break from the game. The ball's gonna drop in forty-five minutes. They've lined up some pretty good music for the show tonight."

They all claimed seats as they awaited the countdown to midnight.

Hunter had taken the recliner, and when he realized Ailis was left without a spot to sit, he grabbed her hand and tugged her onto his lap, tickling her when she tried to get back up.

"Hunter. Stop. There's no room."

"Sure there is. Here." He scooted over and somehow, they managed to share the seat, mostly. They had to twist sideways, so they were watching TV while in a weird, spooning-style position.

Ailis tried to concentrate on the music, tried to work herself out of her snit. She was usually better at shrugging off the dark thoughts, but tonight they were holding fast.

She sighed.

"You're in a foul mood," Hunter mumbled softly, out of earshot of the rest of her family.

"I know. Sorry. New Year's Eve sucks. Gives you too much time for introspection."

"Don't worry, mouse. I'll kiss those bad feelings away at midnight."

She crinkled her nose, pretending that offer held no appeal. Hunter had kissed her only one time. And since then, she'd obsessed over it. Way too much.

Something told her that kiss was going to be the yardstick by which she measured other kisses, and it was going to be a tough one to beat.

"No thanks. I'll just ride it out."

He leaned forward to get a better look at her face. "Man. You *are* a grumpy Gus. Come on." He rose and reached down to help her up as well.

"Where are you guys going?" Finn asked.

"Just grabbing a couple of beers from the kitchen," Hunter said. However, they bypassed the kitchen, walking to her bedroom instead. He closed the door behind them, gesturing that she should sit on her bed, while he claimed a seat on Caitlyn's.

"Let's have it."

She scowled, almost embarrassed by her behavior. She was a total buzzkill. "I'm not fit for company tonight, Hunter. Why don't you go on out and have fun with everybody else? I'm going to crawl into bed, sleep off some of this bitchiness, and try to wake up on the right side of the new year tomorrow."

"You couldn't be bitchy if you tried."

She rolled her eyes. "You, of all people, know better." Somewhere along the line, Hunter Maxwell, the man who used to annoy the shit out of her, had become her best friend. As such, he'd seen her at her very best and her absolute worst this year.

"Stop trying to change the subject. What's rolling around in that head of yours?"

"I lost a whole year to this stupid Paul breakup and I still can't seem to figure out who I am, where I'm supposed to be. I'm floundering like a fish on the shore and it feels like I'm running out of air."

Hunter considered that for a minute, then tilted his head. "Losing and winning isn't always that cut and dry."

"You're saying it's subjective? Because it doesn't feel that way to me. Right now, I'm the big loser."

"I'm saying life *is* winning and losing. Not one or the other."

"Oh." She tried to figure out when Hunter had become the philosophical one in their relationship. "That's true, I guess."

"We're only twenty-eight, A. It's not like we're both walking around with one foot in the grave."

She shrugged. "I can't seem to shake off this mood. I'm feeling very lost, very alone."

Hunter grinned. "Alone? You must have twenty-seven million cousins out there."

She laughed at his exaggeration, even though her family did usually find a way to feel a lot larger than they were. The noise filtering down the hallway was loud, boisterous, fun. "You're doing a terrible job letting me wallow in my pity party."

"That's right. I am. Because you're doing just fine, mouse."

"Okay. I give up. I'm doing fine." And maybe she was. While she'd made zero progress on finding herself, her own career aspirations were faring a bit better lately. In addition to waitressing, she'd started taking on freelance jobs, helping some of the smaller local businesses—Pat's Pub and Hunter's family hotel included—market themselves better. She'd taken out ads and gotten them advertising on some larger internet tourism sites. She felt good going to bat for the little guys, but she still felt that twinge that…something…was missing.

Les, her parents' manager, insisted she was completely screwing up her life. That her calling was staring her right in the face. More than once, he'd demanded that she stop "fucking around" and come on as his partner. He was certain she was made for the world of music—managing the tours while he represented the bands.

For years, she'd denied it, claiming she couldn't face a life spent on the road, even though that had been her original plan when she'd left college. Somewhere along the line, whether it was Paul's influence or her weakness, she had really started to believe she wanted to stay in Baltimore forever. Now she'd had a taste of life without wheels. And while both lifestyles had their pros and cons, it was getting harder and harder to pick which one she preferred.

Rather than accept Les's job offer, she'd appeased him by helping him with his latest venture, *February Stars*. Les had come up with the idea for the talent competition over a year ago. The setup was quite simple. Eight performers would compete for the chance to tour as the opening act for The Universe. Her dad's former band was kicking off their reunion tour at the MGM in National Harbor in April. The entire concert— every show in every city—had been sold out for months. She'd read an article recently that tickets were being resold for as high as six thousand dollars apiece on StubHub.

Les had come up with a list of eight performers he'd been watching, singers with the potential to break big in the business, and he'd dangled his carrot. All eight had signed up for the competition immediately. Who wouldn't? Touring with The Universe would be one hell of a shot at instant stardom.

Les had chosen Baltimore for the contest because, at the time, he'd thought Sky and Teagan would be home in the city. Then they'd gotten an invitation to sing for the Queen of England, and Les decided to set up a mini-European tour for a couple months.

Because Les spent a lot of time on the road, he'd used Ailis as his Baltimore liaison. She'd set up the venue and taken care of permits and anything else that needed to happen locally. Though she hadn't admitted it to anyone, the work had energized her, fulfilled her in a way she'd never experienced.

"So are you feeling any better?" Hunter asked.

She shrugged and dug deep for the response that would appease him. "Yeah. I mean, I suppose there are worse things than spending New Year's with your ugly ass."

"Oh, man. You crossed a line there, Adams." Hunter rose from the bed, approaching her in a threatening manner.

She tried to read his direction, plotting her escape. She glanced toward the door. He'd closed it, which would slow her down too much...

When he got a few steps away, she darted around him, leaping onto Caitlyn's bed, grabbing her pillow as she did so. Hunter gave chase, but now she had a weapon. She swung the pillow at his head as he tried to dodge the blow.

She took that split second to head for the door, but he caught her, pushing her against it. One second, her cheek was pressed against the cool wood, the next, he'd twisted her to face him, holding her hands over her head with one of his.

"Tell me I'm hot," he said.

She snorted. "Yeah, right."

He used his free hand to tickle her. She tried to break free of his grip, even lifting her knee in her desperation. She hated being tickled and he'd left himself vulnerable.

He turned just in time to escape any serious damage to his man parts.

"Bad girl."

"Ha. I wish."

Her joke fell short. For her and, apparently, for Hunter, who released her hands. "What's that mean?"

"Nothing," she hedged, not wanting to admit where her thoughts had gone.

"You want to be a bad girl?"

"Of course not," she said, the response at least eighty-percent lie. "Not really."

He grinned. "Not really?"

"You realize this is all your fault. You keep talking about your twisted love life and teaching me all those slang terms from Urban Dictionary. Thanks a lot for 'felching' by the way. Ew! Everything out of your mouth is sex-related, filthy stuff."

"I keep telling you—filthy is fun."

"See what I mean? It's like you've planted some insidious worm in my brain and now all I can think about is—" She didn't dare finish her comment.

"Kinky sex?"

She sighed. "I used to be such a nice person. Then you came along."

"So now you want to be bad?"

She shrugged. "I think I just want to be interesting."

"Damn. You really don't get it, do you?"

"Get what?"

"You're the most interesting person I've ever met."

She snorted, which was apparently the wrong response, because Hunter, who was never without a smile, actually scowled at her.

"Okay. Now I think I know what your problem is." He walked over to sit on her bed and patted the mattress next to him. "Come here."

She crossed her arms and held her ground.

"Come here, mouse. I just want to talk."

Sadly, she knew that was true. A year had come and gone and Hunter hadn't stepped over the line of friendship except for that brief moment of insanity at the club. She was back to buddy-ville. And while her head knew that was exactly where she should remain, there were times—like now—when her hormones had different ideas.

She dropped next to him on the bed. "What?"

"Do you masturbate?"

"Ugh," she said, bouncing back up from the bed. "What the hell, Hunter?"

"You don't, do you?"

She turned to face him. "I share a room with my cousin. And an apartment with a bunch of other family members. It's not like I have so many opportunities to..."

"Masturbate."

"Please stop saying that word."

Hunter gave her shit-eating grin. "You prefer a better one? Pet the kitty? Flick the bean? Buff the muffin? Polish the pearl?"

Ailis bit her lip, trying hard not to laugh. It was impossible to get into a serious fight with the man because somehow it always ended with her cracking up at some uncouth, crude joke. Tonight, she just wanted to stay mad, something that was getting harder by the minute. "Are you finished? Because I think we should go back out and watch the ball drop."

He shook his head. "Nope. We're staying in here. And making some stuff happen."

She frowned. "Like what?"

Hunter rose from the bed and took her hand. "You think you can turn off your brain for a little while?"

"No."

He laughed. "Yeah. I'm sure you're right, but you're going to have to try, because I have a cure to all that ails you. But you can't overthink it. Hell, you can't think about it at all. You just have to trust me and let go."

Ailis considered his words, trying to figure out how to respond.

Hunter tapped her forehead lightly when her silence lingered too long. "This is what I'm talking about. You want to ask a million questions so you can form some logical, well-thought-out answer. This doesn't work that way."

"So I just have to trust you?"

"Yeah," he said with a nod. "I swear on all that's holy you will feel one million times better afterwards."

She grinned. "I'd settle for ten times better."

"Lay down on the bed."

Five words. He'd only said five words and her brain had already exploded.

He narrowed his eyes slightly, the expression part dare, part I-knew-you-couldn't-do-it. It was effective.

She did as he said, lying on her back, in the middle of her mattress, without question. She tried not to smirk at the definite shock on his face.

If she'd expected him to waver in the face of her unexpected acquiescence, she was destined for disappointment. Instead, Hunter walked to her bedroom door and locked it.

Now it was her turn to react. She closed her eyes, trying not to let him see the tiny bit of panic that was setting in.

"That's not a bad idea," he mumbled softly.

She started to open her eyes to see what he was talking about, but the scarf he'd grabbed from her nightstand was already there, wrapped around her head, robbing her of sight for good.

"I want you to pretend I'm not here, A. Repeat after me. Hunter isn't in the room."

She felt a bit silly, but she said it anyway. "Hunter isn't in the room."

"Before I start, I'm going to make you a promise."

"Okay," she whispered.

"No sex. You've sworn off guys and dating and that's definitely not what this is. So go ahead and kick that worry out of your brain. Okay?"

"Okay," she repeated, simply because she was way out of her element and curious about what he was going to do.

That reticence morphed back to panic when he gripped the waistband of her lounge pants and began to tug them down. Her hands flew to stop him, but he gripped her wrists and pulled them above her head.

"Leave your hands right here. Don't move them."

"Hunter—"

"Isn't here," he said. "Do as I say, Ailis."

She forced herself to remain in the position he'd placed her, trying not to think about how much his power play, his demanding tone, was wreaking havoc on her libido.

He returned to her pants, and this time she didn't offer any resistance as he pulled them and—God help her—her panties off.

She pressed her legs together tightly and tried to twist her lower body away from him, but he didn't give her the chance to hide. Anything.

He gripped the knee closest to him and pulled, moving as he did so to place himself between her outstretched legs.

"So, this sort of goes beyond trust," she said, hating the breathless quality of what she'd intended to be a legitimate complaint.

He silenced her, not with an admonishment, but with a kiss. A quick, hard, unexpected, sexy kiss.

This was getting out of hand. She started to say as much, but before she could lodge her protest, he touched her clit.

Her hips lurched upwards. Jesus. It had been too long since someone had touched her like that, herself included. She tried to suck in a breath, thinking perhaps it was the lack of air reaching her lungs that was impacting her better judgment.

Hunter touched her again, but this time he ran his hand along her slit, the tip of this finger stroking her from anus to clit. Just one soft stroke, but it packed a hell of a punch.

Ailis turned her head to the side, her hands clenched into fists by her head. She'd never found it easy to achieve an orgasm. Sure, she'd had them before, but they generally took some work—on Paul's part and hers. And there had been a lot of nights—too many—when she hadn't managed to get there at all. Toward the end of her relationship with Paul, her climax wasn't even something they really sought. If she got there, great. If not...

Maybe the secret to orgasms was abstinence. She could just go without for long periods of time, and then treat herself to a blowout every three or four years.

Wow. That was a depressing thought.

Hunter touched her clit again, but this time he lingered, rubbed harder, stayed longer. Her hips instinctively followed the path of his finger, lifting to seek more pressure.

She opened her mouth to speak, but didn't know what to say. Did she beg him for more? More what? Touching? Fucking?

She squeezed her eyes together more tightly beneath the blindfold.

This was Hunter. But she was supposed to forget that.

When he slid his fingers lower and slowly pressed one inside her, she stopped giving a fuck who was touching her.

She began to thrust up and down, forcing his finger deeper.

Hunter read her body's unspoken request, adding a second finger to the first, moving faster.

Ailis saw flashes of light behind her closed eyelids. Her hands seemed to move of their own volition to her breasts. She cupped them, squeezed them.

Hunter broke the silence. "Lift your shirt. Grab them harder."

She wasn't sure why she obeyed, but the second he issued the command, she was doing as he said.

"Tug down that bra. Pinch your nipples. Squeeze them tight."

Ailis reacted to the words, dragging the bra beneath her breasts before tightening her forefingers and thumbs around the sensitive nubs. She squeezed harder than she'd ever dared on her own, but the slight pain didn't register as bad. Especially not when combined with Hunter adding a third finger to the two currently sending her to oblivion.

She gyrated on the bed like a mad woman, one giant bundle of nerves, seeking pleasure. His fingers stretched her tight—almost uncomfortably so—but like the pinch on her nipples, it didn't feel bad.

Hunter sealed her fate when he stroked her clit with his thumb, the final blow, the last glorious, holy-fucking-hell straw. Her body hit pleasure overload.

Her back arched as she came, but Hunter pressed it down against the mattress with his body, when he lay on top of her, his mouth capturing her cries with his.

The bliss crashed in on her, wave after wave. Hunter didn't stop kissing her, didn't draw his fingers out until she stilled.

Once she did, he withdrew, then gently pulled her hands away from her breasts, fixing her bra and pulling the shirt down to cover her. Then he put her pants back on. She noticed he didn't bother with the panties, but she didn't care. It wasn't as if she had a leg to stand on when it came to modesty now.

The last thing he did was tug off the blindfold.

She didn't open her eyes. Partly because now that the climax had passed, she was overwhelmed by exhaustion. But also, partly because she was embarrassed to face him.

Ailis wasn't sure why. He'd initiated what they had just done. It had been his idea.

So it wasn't as though she had anything to be ashamed of.

No. It wasn't embarrassment, she realized.

It was something much more dangerous.

She was afraid she'd open her eyes and realize she'd developed serious feelings for Hunter Maxwell.

That couldn't happen. They were a complete mismatch when it came to romance. Ailis wanted forever. Hunter wanted fifteen kinky minutes, horizontal surface optional.

Besides, she wasn't looking for love. She was looking for herself, the woman she never had the chance to become because she was too busy making sure Paul was happy.

"Open your eyes, A."

Her lids fluttered open before she could think about all the reasons she was still hiding. He told her what to do and she did it. That was super annoying, something she was going to have to work on.

He was grinning at her, the same goofy, affable Hunter grin that she had found annoying during the first few years of their acquaintance, but that now sent her heart pitter-patting in a way that told her she'd just epically fucked up.

"Damn, girl. I tried to mute out the majority of that screaming, but when you come, you're loud. Didn't know you had that kind of volume in you."

She narrowed her eyes even as her cheeks heated. All of her cousins were just down the hall, counting down to freaking New Year's.

"You should have thought about that before you...you..."

"Finger fucked you until you went off like a bottle rocket."

She scowled, which only made him laugh.

"Don't act pissed off, mouse, because you're not."

Her shoulders slumped, and she realized she was more relaxed than she had been in weeks. Maybe months. God, she was downright loose, not a bit of stress in her shoulders or neck or anywhere.

"Feel better?" he asked.

She nodded. "Loads."

He rose from the bed and she caught sight of his erection. He noticed where her eyes lingered. "Don't worry about that. Common side effect of watching a beautiful woman coming apart at the seams. Nothing a cold shower won't cure."

She had enough of her wits left to know that wasn't exactly true. And she couldn't help but think it was somewhat selfish of her to take something so amazing from him, then let him walk away still needy and aching.

But the alternative wasn't something she could consider. She couldn't do tit for tat on this. Not with him. She was already struggling to keep her thoughts about him platonic.

She almost snorted aloud at the word *platonic*. She was not having innocent thoughts about Hunter. In truth, she already had them both naked, her legs wrapped around his waist as he pounded deep inside her.

"Hey. Listen," he said, lifting one finger, drawing her attention to the raised voices outside her bedroom door.

"Ten, nine, eight..." her cousins yelled.

"It's almost New Year's."

She sat up on the bed.

"Seven, six, five, four..."

"Yeah," she accepted his hand as he helped her stand on wobbly legs.

"Three, two, one!"

"Happy New Year, mouse," Hunter said.

"Happy New Year."

He bent his head and gave her the least-friendly kiss in the history of New Year's Eve. His kiss proved they'd both crossed a line, one that might be impossible to cross back over.

But because it was Hunter, and he worked on the theory of "do whatever feels good," he didn't bother to hold back.

It was the sexiest, hottest kiss of her life, and it fucked with her world.

When he released her, he pulled away. "Come on. Let's go back to the party. We can play Asshole or teeny-tiny flip cup and get wasted."

And even though Ailis tended to live in the real world most days, as so often happened with Hunter, she followed his lead, letting him drag her into his impulsive good times.

She'd worry about what just happened tomorrow. Tonight, she was too sated, too relaxed, too happy to forget to put up much of a fuss.

"Okay," she agreed. "But you better be prepared to do as I say when you're asshole and I'm president."

"Never gonna happen. I am king of the cards, baby. King. Of. The. Cards."

She rolled her eyes as he laughed and they rejoined the party, slipping back into their "just friends" roles far more easily than she would have imagined.

At least that was what she thought until—two hours later—he bumped into her during a rousing, competitive game of flip cup and she felt the hardness of his cock.

She gave him a curious glance and he leaned close to whisper in her ear, "He's not going away. He likes you."

She was just the right amount of tipsy to laugh at his joke, but whether he was kidding or not, the words stuck.

And her body went soft, her pussy wet. "She likes you too," she murmured, low enough that he couldn't hear.

She'd wished for a change, bemoaned the fact that nothing happened in her life.

Well, something had happened.

Dammit.

Chapter Four

January second dawned gray, drizzly and cold. Ailis wanted to let that affect her mood because she thought she should feel bad. Nothing had changed since New Year's.

Much.

Except she was still feeling pretty chill after the mother of all orgasms.

Mercifully, Hunter had remained at his own apartment yesterday, sleeping off his hangover and "lazing in front of the TV watching football." She had been grateful for the brief break from him. Not that she'd put that time to any great purpose. It wasn't like she'd sorted out her feelings about what they'd done— he'd done to her—the other night. In fact, she was still confused as hell.

The difference was…the sex had done the trick, taken the edge off enough that she didn't really care.

God. She was starting to sound like Hunter. That wasn't a good thing.

"There's my girl."

"Oh my God! Hey, Les. Happy New Year. When did you get into town? I wasn't expecting to see you for another week." Ailis hugged her dad's manager and followed him to the bar.

He grabbed a stool and said, "Hello, Tris."

"Good to see you, Les. Want your usual?" Les was a Scotch man.

Les shook his head. "Just coffee."

Ailis frowned as Uncle Tris poured Les a cup of coffee. Then Tris walked away to make the strawberry daiquiris her table had just ordered.

"Coffee?" she asked. "It's after noon. That's whiskey time."

As she joked, she took a closer look at him. He was a bit pale. "What's wrong? Are you sick?"

Les raised his hand to halt her concerns. "Now don't go getting upset. It's an ulcer."

"Again?" Ailis sighed. "Les, you've got to start taking better care of yourself. Between the smoking, the stress, the booze and the fast food, you're your own worst enemy."

"Thanks so much for the lecture, Teagan Jr."

Ailis grinned. "Bet Mom's been giving you an earful."

"And your dad. I'm taking care of myself, but this one is giving me a run for my money. Doctor wants me to slow down."

She snorted. "Yeah. That'll happen."

"It's happening."

"What?" Ailis didn't bother to hide her surprise. She could count the number of days Les had voluntarily taken off in her entire lifetime with one hand. And she still had fingers left over. That didn't mean he didn't get vacation time. It just meant her parents had to trick him into it occasionally, sending him to the beach or some exotic island under the guise of setting up a performance that wasn't happening, then demanding he stay there under the threat of firing his ass if he booked an earlier return flight.

"I came to Baltimore to recruit you."

"For what?"

"I was hoping you'd be my assistant." He reached for the cup of coffee Tris had set in front of him, but she placed her hand on his arm.

"Coffee isn't any better than whiskey."

Les sighed and put the cup down, looking at it as if he'd just said goodbye to his true love. "Anyway, I'm here because I need your help."

The second he spoke, she remembered. "*February Stars.*"

Les nodded. "Yeah. Starts in a few weeks and shit is hitting the fan. The next time I come up with some great promotional scheme, do me a favor. Kill me before I implement it."

"You've made that request before. Sadly, I'd miss you too much to ever follow through with it."

"I'm worn out, kid. I need some help."

She looked at him and realized he really did look tired. "Maybe you should go back to your hotel to rest. Or you could go upstairs and lay down, stay close so that I can keep an eye on you."

Les patted her cheek affectionately. He'd never married or had kids of his own, which meant for Ailis's entire life, she'd had two loving parents and this man, the doting, spoil-her-and-her-sister-rotten honorary uncle. "You're a good girl."

When she was younger, it was Les who'd kept an eye on her and her sister, Fiona, when her parents performed. They had a nanny, but both preferred to stand in the wings backstage to watch the shows. Ailis loved to listen to Les as he critiqued the performance, making mental notes about what worked and what didn't in terms of costuming, song selection, song placement, band cues and a million other aspects.

As she got older, Les started to ask for her opinion. And she could still remember the first time she'd made a solid suggestion. He made the change in the next show and then bought her the Ugg boots she'd been coveting as "payment" for her "hard work."

After that, she was his shadow, learning everything she could about the business of managing a superstar— or in the case of her parents, two superstars and their band. She credited Les with her decision to major in business and marketing in college.

Of course, she'd broken his heart when she had graduated and taken a job in a marketing firm to be close to Paul rather than join him on the road. He'd made no secret of the fact he thought she would be an excellent tour manager/promoter.

"So it's settled. You need rest." Ailis stood, ready to lead the way upstairs, but Les caught her hand and silently gestured for her to sit back down.

"I'll go up in a minute. Once you give me an answer."

Ailis sat back down, then waved to get Tris's attention. "Do you mind taking those daiquiris to my table, Uncle Tris?"

"No problem," he said, picking up the glasses. "Take your time. It's slow as molasses in January in here this afternoon."

"Probably because it *is* January," she joked.

Tris delivered the drinks and she turned her attention back to Les. "Les—" she started.

"No more excuses, Ailis."

She paused, uncertain how to reply. "What's that supposed to mean?"

"You've been hiding behind that breakup long enough."

"I haven't been hiding."

Les gave her a sad smile. "Sweet pea. Don't kid a kidder. Besides, you know as much about this show as I do. You were in on the planning stages, you know the setup—hell, you put together all the local details. You're the best one to help me run this thing."

February Stars was no small undertaking, and Les knew it. If he was hoping to push her into the world of promotion, this was going to be initiation by fire. Not only would the competition be a live show in a decent-sized venue in Baltimore, Les had worked out a deal to have it broadcast over the Internet as well. So, in addition to the local interest, the performers would be seen worldwide. The exposure for the eight competitors was going to be off-the-charts—win or lose.

"It's only a couple months out of your life. It's not like you've got any other pressing commitments. We'll do it together. I'll deal with the talent and you take care of all the setup stuff, scheduling rehearsals, running some final checks with the accounting firm handling the voting, making sure the venue is prepared for our needs, taking care of ticketing issues."

"You mean all those things you can do in your sleep, ulcer or not?"

Les snorted. "Don't act like you can't do them too. I've been training you for this since you were eight years old. If I didn't have so much damn pride, I'd admit that you could probably do a better job running this whole shebang. But I'm not that magnanimous."

She grinned. "*February Stars* would fall apart without you."

"Maybe. Maybe not. You're bored, angel. You know it and I know it. Even now, I can see that gleam in your eye."

"Did Mom and Dad put you up to this?"

Les went quiet, which was her answer.

"I'm going to get a real job, you know."

"I know, sweetheart. But the fact is *this* should be your real job. You were made for it. And it's not like

I'm leaving you to do it alone. I'm just asking for some help."

"Help you don't really need."

"I'm not lying about the ulcer."

She reached out and grasped his hand. "I know you're not, but the fact is, you spend at least ten months out of every year with an ulcer."

He chuckled. "You're still not answering."

She was hedging. Mainly because her head was whirling over the opportunity. And his words.

Made for this.

Was she?

She was feeling a serious spark of excitement. Something she hadn't felt in a long time. In her head, she knew exactly what needed to be done to make the show a success.

"It's time for you to take charge of your life, kid. You've let your broken heart over that damn doctor hold you back for too long."

Ailis didn't want to admit that was true. Even if it was.

She recalled the way Paul looked at her at the club, and the same anger she'd felt then returned. Not toward him, but toward herself. She'd made Paul her Prince Charming, her Sky Mitchell back in college, convinced he was her happily ever after, her forever.

Looking back now, she realized she'd been settling. He had been the first man to glance her way and not look through her. She had been sitting in the library with Rhonda, forcing her roommate to study for their biology final. Rhonda had been a reluctant study partner, texting more than cramming. Paul, who was in the same class, had joined them at the table and he'd struck up a conversation with her. Not Rhonda. Her.

For a girl who'd never had a boyfriend, never had a guy pay much attention to her, it had been a heady thing.

It had been enough to keep her hanging in there even when it became obvious that Paul was a pretty selfish guy. So much of their relationship, their time together was based on doing what he wanted to do. She let him call the shots, following behind him like a devoted puppy dog. The memory of that made her sick to her stomach these days.

Les reached over and grasped her hand. "If you say no, I'll go it alone. And if I'm lucky, this ulcer won't kill me and I'll still be alive come March."

She laughed. "Jesus, Les. You should have led with that. Saved yourself all the arguing. I'll do it."

Les smiled widely and waved a file in front of her that he pulled out of his briefcase. "Perfect. I'll get copies of this made for you and hand it over tomorrow. It's all the details, contracts, permits, and so on."

The file was easily five inches thick. "Oh my God." She hadn't expected to regret her decision instantly. Instead, she had figured she'd have a few hours before that emotion would wake her up tonight in a cold sweat.

"Oh, and we've got a problem to solve. A big one."

Ailis narrowed her eyes. "I find it interesting you waited until after I agreed to do this to mention the problem."

"Really? You find that interesting?" Les clutched at his heart as if she'd wounded him. "It's like you don't know me at all. I'm a slippery bastard, kid. I thought that was why you loved me so much."

She laughed. "What's the problem?"

"We're down one singer. One of the guys I considered a top contender fell down a flight of stairs. Broke both legs and an arm."

"Oh no!"

"Yeah. I'm sick about it. I was sure he was going to run away with the whole competition. Amazing guitarist."

"I was more concerned about the fall." Leave it to Les to mourn his own loss rather than consider the pain the man must be in.

"Oh…yeah. Sounds like it was an attempted mugging that went bad. Guy in a ski mask jumped him in a dark stairwell of his apartment building late one night. They tussled, and my performer went down a set of concrete stairs pretty hard. Now we're five weeks away and down one singer. I'll never find another performer of the caliber I'm looking for who isn't already booked for February."

"So run the show with seven singers."

Les scowled. "Honey, you know I can't do that. My OCD won't let me start that show with an odd number. I'm already in a lot of pain. That will send me over the top."

If Ailis hadn't just agreed to help him run this damn show, she would have laughed at his comment. Instead, she knew exactly how sincere he was. The man had a weird quirk about odd numbers, which was why there were always two or four backup singers in every show, an even number of band members, an even number of songs in each set. And God help her mom and dad if they ever ended a show with three encores. They'd all but have to sacrifice a chicken the next day to make up for it. "You're insane."

The bell over the door to the pub jingled, capturing her attention.

Hunter walked in—and the light went on.

She knew exactly what type of performer Les was looking for to compete in this show, and Hunter didn't fit the mold. Not even close. Hunter was a pub singer, who'd only seriously started performing nine months ago, after a two-year hiatus. Rhonda dropped her engagement ring by the door and he'd picked up his guitar again. The other competitors had been touring for years, working relentlessly to break into the business.

Regardless, Ailis didn't doubt for a minute that Hunter could give the others a run for their money. He was one of the most talented musicians she'd ever seen. And she'd seen millions of them in her lifetime.

"Hey, mouse," Hunter said, stopping next to her and Les.

"Hunter, you remember Les Fossie, my dad's manager."

Hunter held out his hand and the two men shook.

"Nice to see you again," Les said.

Ailis looked at Hunter, surprised to see him again so soon. "What are you doing here? I thought you had to work."

"I do. But I think my wallet must have fallen out of my pocket the other night in your be—uh, couch. I was going to go look for it."

"Cool." Ailis recalled the way Hunter rocked her world and fought like the devil to keep from blushing. Les was too canny not to notice, and if he did, her next suggestion was going to fail before she uttered it. "Hey, do you think you could perform tonight?"

"Tonight? Um, yeah, sure. I guess. You guys going to start doing music on Mondays now?"

"Possibly," she lied. "We thought we'd give it a try. Seven work?"

He nodded, then headed toward the stairs to her apartment. They rarely locked the door, since it was a safe bet there were always two or three cousins in the pub at any given time.

"So," Les continued as if Hunter hadn't interrupted, "our first order of business is to find another singer."

"I think I already have."

Les gave her a curious look, then his gaze drifted to the apartment door. Hunter was long gone. "The pub singer? Hell no. Ailis, you know what kind of performers I'm looking for."

"Let him audition. Tonight."

"Ailis, honey, be reasonable. That competition will be cutthroat. I've got singers who've been on the road for years."

"And they still haven't made it big. *February Stars* is about promoting up-and-comers. Sounds like you've loaded the slate with been-around-the-blockers."

Les scowled. "Very funny. I've loaded the slate with experience and talent because that's what the prize calls for. Whoever wins is hitting the road, opening for The Universe on tour. I can't hand that over to someone whose primary experience is singing in a pub."

"All I'm asking you to do is listen to him. He is one of the most talented singer-songwriters I've ever met. Trust me. He has the voice, the look and the drive to succeed. If you put him in this show, you won't regret it. Not for one second."

"Ailis..." He was still resistant.

"Putting him in the contest doesn't mean he'll win. This will serve two purposes. Get Hunter some of that experience you claim he needs and even up your numbers. Would it be a terrible thing to have any of the other seven singers win and hit the road with The Universe?"

"No. I picked them because they were all performers I could live with, ones I knew could handle the stress of the road. Honey, the chances of him making it to the second round are nil."

"Then what do you have to lose other than your problem being solved?"

Les sighed, clearly hesitant.

"Tell you what. You can go upstairs and take a nap. You really do look like shit. And then, come down for a healthy dinner and listen to some music. If you like what you hear, we've got our eighth performer. If you don't, we've only lost a few hours and I'll start beating the bushes tomorrow to continue the search."

Les stood, and she was struck once more by how weary he looked. She struggled to recall when Les had gotten old. She didn't like to think of him aging, and right now, he looked twenty years older than Pop Pop, who was a very spry ninety-two.

"I'll listen to the pub singer. And then, tomorrow, we'll start a serious search."

"Okay."

"And, Ailis," Les said, turning back toward her. "That thing you just did, to convince me to listen to Hunter sing? That's what I'm talking about. You were made for this life. Time to stop fighting the inevitable."

She didn't reply. Instead, she watched Les climb the stairs and then she waited for Hunter to come back down. She was torn between telling him that tonight was an audition or keeping it a secret, lest he get too nervous.

His chances of actually getting into the show were probably slim to none. Les was a stubborn bastard, set in his ways. He knew what he wanted, and swaying him—even with someone as talented as Hunter—was going to be tough. So was it right to let Hunter get his hopes up?

On the other hand, Hunter had more than a healthy amount of competitive spirit. If he knew what was at stake, there was a very good chance he'd kill it.

He finally reappeared and her decision to tell him was made the second she looked at his clothes. He was dressed in saggy jeans that should have been washed at least two weeks earlier and an ancient T-shirt he found at Goodwill with a faded picture of Christopher Walken that said, "More Cowbell."

Image mattered, and she was going to fix his.

"Hey, Tris," she said, looking at her uncle. "I'm off the clock in an hour. Since it's so slow, do you mind if I take off early?"

Tris shook his head. "No, I'm good."

"If things pick up, Sunnie is upstairs and I know she'd pitch in. Oh, and..." She considered the file folder Les had shown her.

"I already heard. Congrats on the new gig. I'll tell Ewan to leave you off the work schedule for the foreseeable future. Hopefully forever."

"You go to hell for eavesdropping," she teased.

"Sweetheart, it's not eavesdropping that's gonna send me there," he said with a wink.

She laughed. "By the way, you might want to tell Ewan to call in a couple of extra waitresses for tonight."

"What do you have planned?" Tris asked.

"You'll see," she said as Hunter walked up to her.

"Found it," Hunter said, waving his wallet.

"Can you take today off work?" she asked.

He shrugged. "I guess. Why?"

"Call your uncle. We have a lot to do and not much time."

"Ailis," he said. "What are you talking about?"

"You remember me telling you about *February Stars*?"

He nodded. "That's the talent competition you've been helping your dad's manager with, right?"

"Yeah. We're down a singer. Tonight is your audition."

Hunter didn't move, didn't make a single sound for a full minute. "I thought this competition was between

74

experienced singers, performers who'd been at it for a while?"

"It is. Was. One of the guys broke his legs and an arm. It's last minute, so replacing him is going to be tough. A lot of the performers we have in the competition committed nearly a year ago because they travel and have touring schedules."

He didn't reply, so she kept talking.

"You're good, Hunter. Really good. I know you haven't been at it as long, but that doesn't mean you don't have the talent to pull this off. If I didn't believe you could enter that competition and seriously compete, I wouldn't have mentioned your name."

Hunter had been in a band all through high school and into his early twenties. Then Rhonda complained about how often it took him away from her and he quit. Since the breakup, he'd been performing solo, primarily at the pub and the occasional gig at smaller local venues.

"You know you're the only person who really believes that, Ailis. Everyone else just thinks I'm goofing off."

"I think people are afraid to go for their really big dreams. It's easier to shrug things off as impossible than to put themselves out there and try."

He grinned. "Are you calling me a coward?"

"Not at all. I'm saying you're different."

"How so?"

"Because you're not a coward. You're not afraid to dream big. And you've also got an amazing work ethic. You'll do what it takes. I know it."

He still seemed hesitant, so she continued, "If you really want this, Hunter, it's time to put your money where your mouth is. You're going to kill it at this audition tonight. And then you're going to win that competition. And then you're going to go on tour with The Universe, record a million gold records, and that is when the entire world is going to see exactly what I see." She waggled her fingers, jazz-hands style. "Superstar!"

Hunter reached out before she realized his intention and tugged her toward him, wrapping her up in a giant bear hug. "I don't think I've ever thanked you, mouse."

"For what?"

"For cheering me up a year ago when I crashed into your apartment, intent on killing Paul. For giving me the singing gig here—I know you were the one who talked Tris into hiring me. For what you just said about me being talented, and for believing in me. And about a million other things. I keep thinking this last year sucked, but now, I'm not so sure it did. That probably sounds dumb."

She shook her head, his words soaking in, making sense. She had been miserable since Paul left. And at the same time, she'd been happy too, having fun with her cousins and with Hunter. It wasn't the future she had imagined, and there was still some big stuff to work out—her career and her love life—but for now, she was footloose and fancy free and that wasn't as horrible as she liked to pretend. "No, it doesn't sound dumb. I get it. I really do. But, Hunter..."

"Yeah?"

"That T-shirt and those jeans are garbage. Stuff that wallet back in your pants. We're going shopping. You and I are about to create your new image."

Two hours later, Ailis looked up from her phone as Hunter walked out of the dressing room of the fifth shop they'd visited.

Her mouth fell open. "Oh yeah. Finally. What do you think? How does that feel?"

Hunter, whose patience had faltered somewhere between the third and fourth store, replied, "I think what I thought about all the rest of the outfits. It's fine."

She stood up and waved her finger, indicating he should turn around. He did so without complaint, which was an improvement from the first two shops.

"I'm really not enjoying this reverse *Pretty Woman* thing we've got going on," he said once he was facing her again.

She grinned but ignored him, her gaze locked on his outfit. She'd paired new slim-fit cuffed jeans with an untucked dark gray button-down shirt that sported a funky, but low-key black pattern and topped it with a fitted blazer. "It's perfect."

Hunter looked in the full-length mirror. "You think so?"

"Absolutely. A bad boy Prince Harry. A heartbreaker. But not the scary variety. The sexy JT type. Do me a favor. Don't shave when you get home. You've got just the right amount of scruff going on. It adds to the look."

Her phone beeped and she glanced at the screen.

"Who have you been texting all day?"

"Just some people. I'm trying to set some stuff up."

"So I'm buying this getup?"

She nodded. "Definitely. Okay, so now that we've nailed down your look, we need to figure out your set. Song selection is going to be crucial, because I doubt Les will sit through more than the first two or three numbers if he's not wowed. So we've got to make those songs count. *February Stars* is going to be a mix of covers and original material, so we should work that angle tonight. Start with a familiar showstopper, then move on to your strongest original, which is—"

"'Her Eyes'," they both said in unison.

Ailis laughed. "Well, I guess that's decided. So now we just need to figure out your first song."

"Would it be sucking up to sing your parents' biggest hit?"

"'Maybe Tomorrow'?" Ailis considered the suggestion. The song was originally a duet, but it had been remade several times over the past thirty years in a wide variety of arrangements. She'd actually heard Hunter's version before. It was incredible. "I think that's a great idea. I love the way you've reworked it. Made it faster, grittier."

"So it's happening."

Ailis tilted her head. "Are you nervous?"

Hunter shrugged. "I wasn't until about five seconds ago. You've done a great job distracting me all day." He glanced at the time on his phone. "Shit, is it that late?"

Ailis leaned forward to look and winced as well. "You don't have time for a freak-out right now. Tell you what? I'll get a cab back to my place. You run home, change, grab your guitar and I'll meet you back at the pub in an hour."

Hunter nodded. "Yeah. Okay."

"Hey," she said, gripping his forearm. "You're going to be great."

His smile grew, and then, like on New Year's Eve, he shocked her when he bent down and kissed her. Unlike that night, this kiss was quicker. Less passion and friendlier.

"You keep kissing me," she said, eyes narrowed.

"That one was for luck."

"Oh. Okay. Well then, break a leg."

He chuckled, paid for the clothing, and they parted ways on the sidewalk.

By the time Ailis returned to the pub, she'd managed to work herself up into her own mini panic attack. Not only was she nervous for Hunter, but what she'd agreed to take on was slowly beginning to sink in as well. Helping to organize an event the size of

February Stars was going to be a shit-ton of work, even with Les at the helm.

She was two steps inside Pat's Pub when her phone rang.

"Hey, Mom," Ailis said as she answered.

"Hi, sweetheart."

"Where are you now?" Ailis had seen an itinerary of her parents' tour before they left, but there'd been too many cities to keep track.

"We're spending a couple of days in Tuscany before popping over to Barcelona. It's so beautiful here, babe. Wish you could have come with us."

"I don't remember getting an invite."

Her mother didn't respond for a moment. "Would you have come? I'd gotten the impression lately that you were tired of the hustle and bustle of touring."

Shit. She couldn't deny that. Chalk up another mark in the loss category. She'd missed out on a fantastic European trip and a chance to meet the freaking Queen thanks to her lack of backbone while under Paul's influence.

"I'm kidding," she lied. "There was no way I could leave this glamorous job waiting tables at the pub."

"Doesn't sound like you'll have to do that for much longer. Les just told us the exciting news!"

"Exciting? Is that what we're calling it?" she joked.

"Of course we are. Your dad and I are thrilled you're finally pursuing your calling."

Ailis rolled her eyes, grateful her mother wasn't there to see her. Her parents, like Les, had always thought she was made for a career in music. Not the singing kind. The managing kind.

"Mom, you guys set me up, so you can stop pretending otherwise."

"You're intelligent and creative, Ailis. It's time to stop hiding in that pub and get out, do something with your life."

Wow. Talk about a theme. "It's only been a year." She grimaced even as she said it. A whole freaking year. "I'm going to figure it all out, Mom. Honest."

"I know you will. And I'm sorry for the speech. I worry about you, love. It feels like everyone in the world can see your potential except for you. Paul was only too happy to let you support him without ever giving you a chance to truly shine."

"Did you always feel that way about him?"

Mom paused for several heartbeats. "Not as strongly as I did after he ran off with that woman. I guess I saw it, but you always seemed so happy and in love."

"I was an idiot."

"No, you weren't. He was your first love. We all do stupid things when we're in love."

"You didn't."

"I got lucky. I think in the end you'll be a stronger, smarter woman because you'll go into your next relationship with your eyes wide open. Just make sure you don't lose sight of what *you* want and need as well."

Her mom was always good with the pep talks.

"I will. Thanks, Mom. Look, I hate to do this, but I really have to go. I've got a slew of things to take care of."

"Hunter's audition."

"Les told you about that?"

"Yeah, he said he only agreed to listen because you were so insistent and earnest. I don't want you to be disappointed if it doesn't work out."

Ailis appreciated her mother's concern, but the only thing about this entire venture she was certain about was Hunter's participation in the competition. Her mom and Les had never heard him sing, didn't realize the incredible talent Pat's Pub had been harboring.

She'd heard him playing with his band with Paul on occasion, and she'd always thought he had a great voice. However, it wasn't until he'd picked up the guitar again and started playing solo that Ailis had recognized his true potential.

Apparently, he'd been writing songs for most of his life, but since the breakup, he'd penned a ton of them, called it "his therapy." They were amazing—stories set to music, full of emotion and poetry—and they really showcased his voice, the rich tone, the deep flavor of it. "It's going to work out. Hunter deserves to be in the competition. Les will see that in an instant."

Mom chuckled softly. "And you still think you weren't made to be a manager."

"I really do have to go."

"Okay. Text me later to tell me how it went."

"Will do." Ailis disconnected and glanced around the pub. There was already a pretty good crowd gathering. Her texting had done the trick. While Hunter had spent the afternoon trying on clothes, she'd sent out invitations to everyone in her contacts list in an attempt to build up the audience for tonight's audition.

While she didn't doubt Hunter's talent and new look would be enough, she also knew the power of fans. Making sure Les saw how much the pub patrons loved Hunter could only help her friend's odds.

"Do we have you to thank for this sudden rush?" Padraig asked as she approached the bar.

"Yeah. Sorry. Should have called to warn you."

Padraig shrugged. "No worries. We just rallied the troops upstairs. They all wanted to be down here anyway to see Hunter's audition."

"How do you all... Uncle Tris?" she asked.

"If you don't specify something as a secret, that makes it gossip and fair game in this family."

"How could I have forgotten?" Hunter's audition wasn't a secret, but she hoped he didn't lose his cool when he saw the crowd gathering. She probably should have warned him to expect a packed house. Typically, Monday evenings were slower. Tonight was clearly the exception.

"Hey, I'm going to reserve a table for Les. Okay?"

"Of course." Padraig came out from behind the bar, and the two of them tried to decide which table provided the best vantage point. Once it was selected, she put a cardboard placard on it, declaring it off-limits.

With that last item attended to, she hovered near the front door, waiting.

The butterflies in her stomach grew more aggressive, more restless. At first, she thought her nervousness was on Hunter's behalf, but she realized quickly it was for her.

He'd become a really good friend, someone she relied on more than she cared to admit. If everything went as well as she hoped, this truly could be his big break. His shot at stardom.

Which left Ailis trying to figure out if tonight was going to be the beginning of something big.

Or the end of something she didn't want to lose.

Chapter Five

Hunter closed his eyes briefly as his second song came to a close. The crowd—Jesus, was everyone in Baltimore here tonight?—cheered loudly. Ordinarily that sound energized him, pumped him up. Tonight, it may as well have been white noise, an annoying, meaningless buzz in the background.

He'd purposely avoided looking at Ailis. She was sitting with Les, the man who held far too much power over Hunter at the moment. This man could make or break him. And while the reasonable part of him knew this was only one audition, that there would be other chances, right now, all Hunter could feel was the unbearable weight of all or nothing.

Unfortunately, Ailis was usually his go-to in the crowd whenever he was singing. He'd catch her gaze as she was waiting tables, and her smile would encourage him to try that little bit harder. Tonight, however, he deprived himself of her face, too afraid of what he would see there.

However, he was two songs in. Which meant it was time to face the devil. As he started playing the next tune, he forced himself to look at Ailis's table. She and Les were leaning close to each other, deep in a very serious conversation. Ailis nodded, and then stood at the same time Les did.

He was leaving. He'd only stayed for two songs.

Hunter forced himself to start singing, grateful he'd picked "Brown Eyed Girl." He could sing the song in his sleep he'd played it so many times. Plus, the crowd never failed to join in, which meant he could let them carry it if his voice faltered. Which he feared it might. Disappointment was closing in, crushing him.

Ailis walked Les to the door. That was as far as Hunter would let his gaze travel before staring at the wall in front of him. He didn't want to see the disappointment on Ailis's face. He felt like a big enough failure without having to acknowledge that he'd let her down as well.

He kept singing, his eyes focused solely on the old Irish Whiskey advertisement someone had framed and hung there about a million years ago. Hunter was grateful when he neared the end of the song. He had only played three, but he was done. There was no way he could push himself to finish the set.

That was when Ailis stepped in front of the picture that had been his saving grace. She blocked his view of the ad, giving him an exasperated look. Then she threw her hands up in a classic "what the fuck" gesture that clued him into the fact she'd obviously been trying to capture his attention.

The song ended and he paused, uncertain what to do next as he stared at Ailis.

She put him out of his misery with one brighter-than-the-sun smile and two thumbs up.

"You're in," she mouthed.

And the entire night shifted. Just like that.

His nerves vanished, replaced with a joy so big he was surprised there was enough space in the pub to hold it all. Suddenly, with the change in his attitude, the atmosphere in the room changed from somewhat stifling, to party of the century. He was flying high as he belted out song after song. Everyone sang along, getting louder, growing livelier. It felt like Thanksgiving, Christmas and New Year's Eve all rolled together.

Ailis started waiting tables, delivering pints of Guinness and Natty Boh and shots of Jameson.

His gaze kept returning to hers as she laughed and sang along and even shimmied through the tables, much to her customers' delight. She was so different from the woman he'd known back when she'd dated Paul.

He'd always thought of her as this quiet, shy wallflower, hovering so far in the background it was easy to forget she was there. Paul commanded all the attention and Ailis was just sort of a shadow.

Nowadays, she was all he could see. It was weird. Every time he walked into a room, she was the first thing his eyes focused on. It was as if she had some beacon strapped to her, shooting out this bright light that blinded him to everyone and everything else.

He brought the set to a close, thanking everyone for coming out. "I appreciate your willingness to face Tuesday morning with a hangover just to support me."

As he packed up his guitar, several women came over to the stage, one of them carrying a beer. He was used to this. Hell, he enjoyed this part. Women liked musicians. He'd figured that out in high school, hence the garage band. He used his guitar to pick up women the way some men used cars or corny lines or expensive gifts. Ailis called them his groupies, giving him shit for getting carried away with their attention.

Unlike his quiet best friend, Hunter wasn't as good at denying himself physical pleasure. Ailis insisted on love and commitment and forever. Hunter was just fine with thirty minutes and the backseat of a car.

However, tonight, there was only one person he wanted to celebrate with. And she just happened to be walking by with an empty tray. "Excuse me a minute," he said to the three women jostling for position and the shot at getting him into bed.

"Hey, Ailis. You got a minute?"

Ailis glanced at the three women and smirked. "I think the real question is, do you?"

He didn't have a chance to reply before the boldest of the three women called out to him, "Why don't the four of us continue the party at my place, Hunter?"

Hunter turned around in surprise, studying the women. They weren't fighting for dibs? What the hell were they offering? An orgy?

He leaned closer to Ailis, whispering in her ear, "I just need a minute."

If she was surprised by his request, she didn't show it. "I'm going to steal him away for a second, girls. Hunter and I need to talk business."

Ailis took his hand and guided him toward the back hallway that led to the restrooms. He noticed none of the women put up a fuss or looked very concerned. Apparently, they didn't consider Ailis a threat.

Ailis tugged him into a storage room, turned on the light and shut the door.

"Thanks. I needed a minute to catch my breath."

She frowned, looking confused, and he knew why. He never walked away from a beautiful woman, let alone three.

"You know I won't hold you to that no-dating thing if you really want to go home with those women. I really only made that vow for me. I didn't mean you had to deprive yourself of fun as well."

"I'm cool."

He wasn't. He'd been struggling to get his bearings since New Year's. He had done what he always did that night, rolled with a feeling, let his gut drive him. Ailis had been tense and horny as hell, even if she wouldn't admit it.

For some insane reason, he'd thought he could take care of that problem without it affecting him. Jesus. What a fucking joke. He'd spent the better part of yesterday on his couch with a hard-on that wouldn't go away no matter how many times he jerked off.

Then he realized something he'd never really considered before. Ailis was gorgeous, sexy, hot as hell. She had inherited her mom's long, silky red hair and she had this shy smile—one she often tried to hide behind her hand—that took his breath away. It was easy to overlook her appearance because, like everything else about Ailis, she somehow found a way to make herself smaller. That had never bothered him until he'd seen the way Paul had looked at her at the club. And the way those three women had let her take him away without a word of complaint.

He didn't like the way she pretended to be invisible. He had met her nine years ago, when she and Paul were still just friends in college, and until this last year, he'd never once realized how smart, how funny, how fucking beautiful she was. It was like she pulled a veil over herself.

Now that he thought about it, she was still doing that. She hadn't considered for one second that he might turn those women down for her.

Dammit, she was there the other night. She knew he'd walked around for an uncomfortable amount of time with a fucking hard-on in his pants, wanting her. How could he not? Her responses to him when he'd lain her down on that stupid tiny bed were so much more than he'd expected. He'd actually thought she might be a little repressed when it came to sex. Instead, he'd been introduced to sex incarnate. She was open, daring, passionate and, God help him, submissive. Try as he may, he still couldn't wrap his head around that detail.

"You do know what they're offering you out there, right?"

He scowled. "What do *you* think?"

"So you know that, and you *still* wanted to escape? Why? Isn't that sort of a guy's ultimate fantasy? Three girls at once?"

He grinned, forcing himself to get them back to something resembling normal. Ever since that kiss in the club, he'd been fighting like the devil to keep his growing desire for her in check. Regardless of the definite chemistry, he and Ailis were about as different as two people could get. Losing Rhonda had been tough, but he'd bounced back. Something told him if he ever crossed the line with Ailis, and things didn't work out, losing her would be devastating...and recovery wouldn't come easy, if at all. "I'm not going to pretend I'm not flattered by your high opinion of my stamina and sex drive."

She snorted. "Shit. I just inflated that oversized ego even more."

Hunter ignored her jest, changing the subject to something safer. "So Les liked the songs?"

"Oh, God! Of course, you want to know what he said. He liked the songs just fine, but what he really loved was *you*. Your voice, the image, the whole thing. He was completely blown away."

"But he only stayed for two songs."

Ailis smiled. "He'd already decided after the first one."

"Damn," Hunter muttered, floored by her words and overwhelmed with more happiness than any person could cram into a single body.

"Hmph," she huffed. "I'm going to pretend I'm not insulted that you didn't take *my* word for how great you are, but instead had to hear it from someone else."

Hunter laughed at her fake annoyance. "I apologize for not trusting your opinion, mouse. I mean it's obvious you've got my number. From my talent to my sex drive, I'm an open book to you."

"You're an arrogant asshole."

"And you're a good friend." Even as he said it, that word felt wrong. She was so much more than a friend. But he couldn't put any other word out there in the universe. They were already on shaky ground.

Ailis flushed slightly. He was used to her blushing whenever anyone paid her a compliment, but he wasn't expecting the visceral, punch-to-the-gut reaction he had to it this time.

"So, what are you going to do about the groupies? They're still waiting for you."

Hunter tried to read her look. Was she jealous? Was she as fucked up as he was after the other night?

Ever since the night Rhonda and Paul had dumped them, he'd become…what? He tried to think of a word. The best he could come up with was protective. He was getting tired of people looking through Ailis. It pissed him off.

"They can wait all night. I'm not going anywhere with them."

"Want me to shoo them away? Make an excuse for you?"

He shook his head. "I don't need a fake excuse. I already have a reason for staying right here."

"And what's that?"

"You're here." That was all he said before he bent down to kiss her. Again.

He'd opened the floodgates at the club, and since then, the memory of his lips on hers was all he could think about. He'd chalked that first kiss up to impulsiveness and stupidity. Two things he excelled at.

Ailis had accepted his kiss that night without complaint. He figured that acquiescence was half shock, half saving face in front of Paul. On New Year's, she'd gone along with the game, pretended it wasn't him. And this afternoon, she'd rolled with his kiss at the store, probably because he'd kept it short and downplayed the desire behind it.

This time, the shock value was gone.

She pressed against his shoulders, forcing him away. "What the hell are you doing?"

"I think that's pretty obvious. I'm kissing you."

"But why?"

"Because I want to."

"But what about those women? I thought—"

He wiped away whatever else she might say with another kiss—this one harder, more demanding. Her lips parted on a gasp and he took advantage, rubbing his tongue against hers. Ailis responded briefly before her brain got in the way again.

She twisted her face away from him. "Hunter. Stop. The other night, when you—"

Before she could finish her statement, the door to the storage closet opened and Padraig walked in. Neither he nor Ailis missed the shock on her cousin's face.

"What the hell's going on in here?" Padraig asked, when he spotted what obviously looked like Hunter making unwanted advances.

Ailis tried to shrug out of Hunter's grip, which prodded him to tighten his hold. She wasn't getting away from him that easily. "Oh thank God, Paddy. Hunter just attacked me. Beat him up."

"Attacked you?"

Hunter rolled his eyes. "By 'attack,' she means I kissed her."

Padraig looked at Hunter, scowling. "Why are you kissing her?"

Hunter glanced at Ailis, who was still fighting tooth and nail to free herself from his arms. Her face was flushed and her lips plump, wet, inviting. "Because she needs to be kissed. A lot."

Padraig looked from Hunter to Ailis and back again, then he chuckled. "Yeah. I think you're right. Carry on."

Ailis's mouth fell open as her cousin grabbed the case of beer he'd come for and opened the door.

"You're going to leave me here alone with him? Where's that overprotective bullshit you and every other Collins male exerts whenever some guy comes sniffing around?"

Padraig shrugged as he pointed at him. "That's not some guy. It's Hunter. And he's right. You *do* need to be kissed."

With that, Padraig left, closing the door behind him.

Hunter lost no time taking advantage of the opportunity. He kissed her again, cupping her cheeks, loving the way she stopped trying to push him away.

Instead, her hands found their way around his neck, allowing him to lower his arms to pull her body more fully against his.

Hunter was acutely aware of Ailis's breasts and her tiny waist and her firm ass.

She gasped when he cupped her ass cheeks, renewing her fight once more. "Dammit, Hunter! You're going to have to explain what it is you're hoping to accomplish here."

Hell if he knew. He wasn't like Ailis. He didn't think things through to their logical conclusions prior to taking the first step. He flew by the seat of his pants, jumped in with both feet and hoped there was enough water to soften the impact.

He was kissing her because he'd discovered she was a good kisser. And he wanted her. Which was probably going to be problematic, considering her ban on men and his desire for a rock star lifestyle. Something Ailis said she didn't want, though every time those words crossed her lips, he heard Paul's voice speaking them.

But because those realizations were counterproductive to what he wanted right now, he ignored them. "Do we have to figure this out, mouse? Why can't we just enjoy ourselves for a little while?"

"I have no idea how to do that."

She didn't mean her comment as a joke, but he laughed anyway. Because he knew she was telling the truth. Spontaneous wasn't her style. The most impulsive thing she'd ever done was quitting her job, but even with that, he suspected she'd simply put the pieces together faster than most mere mortals could have with a freshly broken heart. She couldn't have continued working with Rhonda. That was a no-brainer. Rather than hem and haw, she'd cut the cord, which was the practical, logical answer.

"Why are you laughing? I'm being serious."

Hunter slipped his hands to her hips, holding her in place, unwilling to let her take even one step away from him. "I know you are. It's not in you to lie. Which is why I'm going to give you the truth as well. I have no idea why I'm kissing you. All I know is I like it. I like the way you taste, the way you smell, the way you feel in my arms. I can't really give you any more of an answer than that."

"The way I smell?"

"Coconut and apples."

"Oh. Yeah. I ran out of shower gel before shampoo. Decided to switch up scents."

He leaned down to kiss the top of her head. "Do we have to have a reason besides the ones I gave you?"

She looked up at him and for a second, he thought he was going to win. He should have known better.

"Yes. We do. Do you want to date me?"

Did he? He hadn't really considered such a thing. Given the fact he'd just been handed his dream come true on a platter career-wise, he wasn't sure embarking on a relationship was such a great idea. He needed to concentrate on the competition.

"I don't know," he hedged, employing the old toss-the-question-right-back method. "Do you want to date *me*?"

She shook her head. "Hell no. You're a womanizer. A player. A musician with three groupies waiting outside that door to go do some sort of orgy shit."

He would have laughed at her orgy comment if he wasn't so pissed off by the rest. "Nice to know you think so highly of me."

"See," she said, trying to break free of his grip. He didn't let go. "This is what I mean, Hunter. Things that don't bother us as friends would drive us nuts if we were dating. You view commitment as if it's the plague."

"Better that than your approach to relationships. You can't spend five minutes alone with a single man without cataloguing all his pros and cons and analyzing whether or not he's husband material. Every date doesn't have to end with a marriage proposal."

"I don't do that."

"You kind of do," he said, still feeling the need to defend his honor. "You know I don't fuck every woman I go out with."

She lifted her eyebrows haughtily. "You kind of do."

"Right, so no more kissing. Got it."

Hunter let go of her, stepping away to give her room to walk to the door.

He expected her to storm out, but instead, she turned to look at him. "Are we in a fight?"

Just like that, the steam cooled. He shook his head. "No, mouse. We're not."

"So you're not mad at me?"

Her question was one hundred percent Ailis. She hated confrontations, hated thinking someone she cared about was upset with her. And as much as her words stung, he wasn't going to lie and deny there wasn't some truth behind them. Not as much as she thought, but that wasn't her fault. He'd spent the better part of the last year bragging about his conquests to her. If she thought he was a player, it was because he'd painted the damn picture for her.

"Not even a little bit mad."

"Good. Because we have a ton of work to do to get you ready for this competition."

"Are you allowed to help me?"

"Les fired me as his assistant before you hit the first chorus of 'Maybe Tomorrow'. He insisted I help you instead. All the other competitors have agents. He said it wouldn't be fair if you didn't have the same."

"Is that going to be a conflict of interest? I mean, your folks are sort of the prize."

She shrugged. "I don't know. I'll mention that to Les. I mean, it's not like I can really sway the results of the contest in any way. The winner is selected by the fans. They're voting with an app and the results are going through an accounting firm. Management has zero control over the outcome. I'll be honest, Hunter, Les doesn't..." She hesitated.

"He doesn't think I'll make it beyond the first show, so he figures what's the harm in letting you help, right?"

She nodded. "Plus, me helping you sort of serves his purpose more than me being his assistant."

"How so?"

"It's giving me a chance to manage talent. Something Les insists is my calling."

Hunter considered the way she'd helped him all day. "I don't think he's wrong about that."

She snorted. "God, not you too."

"I'm glad Les is cool with it because I really want—no, I *need* your help. Desperately."

"It's yours. As long as you stop kissing me."

He rolled his eyes, walking toward her, getting a kick out of the way she watched his approach with equal parts alarm and desire. They might not be compatible personality-wise, but physically, there was definitely a powerful pull. He bent down until his face was only a few inches from hers.

"I'm not going to make any promises about that."

She released an exasperated breath. "Even after everything we just discussed."

"What can I say? You're a thinker. I'm a doer." And to prove that point, he planted one more hard kiss on her lips before leaving her alone in the storage room.

By the time she emerged, the flush in her cheeks had faded, and he'd given the three groupies the brush-off.

"Hunter Maxwell?" a man seated at a table near the front said, capturing not only his attention, but Ailis's.

"Yeah."

"Congratulations on the competition." The man wasn't sitting alone. He shared the table with another guy with long hair pulled back in a ponytail, a serious rocker chick with long jet-black hair and quite a bit of ink, and a Taylor Swift wannabe with a small dog in a purse on her lap.

Ailis pointed to the dog and the woman clutched it closer. "Emotional support pet," she spat out.

"Okay," Ailis said. "Would he like a bowl of water?"

The woman relaxed her grip, her scowl fading. "No. Thank you."

"Do I know you?" Hunter asked the man who'd spoken to him.

The man shook his head. "No, but you're going to." He stood and held out his hand. "I'm Victor Rodriguez. And these are my friends, Robbie Pierson, Rory Summit, and Leah Valladares. We're in the *February Stars* competition as well."

Hunter shook Victor's hand as he studied all their faces again. Robbie and Leah appeared curious about him, while Rory looked downright bored. "Nice to meet you."

"What are you doing here?" Ailis asked.

"Checking out the competition," Victor explained. "Les told my agent this afternoon he was holding an audition for the last spot. We thought we'd come give you a listen since none of us has ever heard of you."

"You're Sky Mitchell's daughter, aren't you?" Leah asked.

Ailis nodded. "Yes, I am."

Leah gave Victor an "I told you so" look that instantly put Hunter's back up. "Guess that explains that."

"I'm sorry?" Hunter said.

Victor smirked. "We couldn't figure out how a nobody pub singer landed a spot in the competition. Looks like all he had to do to get his big break was fuck Sky's daughter."

One minute, Victor was standing in front of him. The next he was sprawled out on the floor. Hunter couldn't recall throwing the punch, but given the way Tris and Padraig were pulling him away from the man, it was apparent he had.

Ewan had come over from Sunday's Side and he was helping Victor to his feet. "I think it would be a good time for you and your friends to clear out of here."

"Why us?" Victor snarled. "He's the one who threw the punch."

"Defending my niece's honor," Ewan explained. His expression was deadly. Her cousin and uncles had heard the insult.

Robbie, who'd been quiet through the entire melee, rose from his seat and gestured toward the exit. "Come on, guys," he urged the others. "Let's go." He glanced at Ewan. "We don't want any trouble."

"Then I suggest you not come back," Ewan said softly.

Robbie nodded and walked out with Victor and the blonde with her damn dog, while the rocker chick held back.

Tris and Padraig didn't loosen their grip until the trio was completely out of the pub.

"I'm okay," Hunter said. "You can let go."

"Pretty sure holding you back is the only thing keeping *me* from going after that son of a bitch myself," Padraig said.

"Oh sure," Ailis said, throwing her hands up. "*Now* you're willing to fight to the death for me. Where was that response twenty minutes ago in the storage closet?"

Padraig grinned, while the expressions on Tris's and Ewan's faces darkened. Hunter might have dodged a bullet with the cousin, but the uncles wouldn't be as easy to sidestep.

"What about the storage closet?" Ewan asked.

Ailis appeared to regret her words, forgetting her uncles were still there and listening. "Nothing. It was nothing."

For a tense minute, Hunter thought her uncles would demand an explanation. However, when neither she nor Padraig appeared ready to offer one, they returned to their respective sides of the business—Tris stepping back behind the bar, while Ewan resumed his duties in the restaurant.

Padraig chuckled. "Man, thanks for spicing up a boring Monday night, Ailis."

"Go away, Paddy," she said, her words lacking any heat. He took his place next to his dad behind the bar.

"Sorry about that," the rocker chick said after the others walked away. "My gut told me to turn down Victor's invitation when he called this afternoon— mainly because the guy's a total douchebag—but I wanted to hear you sing. You're really good. You deserve a spot in the contest."

Hunter smiled, then he recognized her and his eyes widened. "Holy shit. You're Rory Summit."

Rory laughed. "Yeah, I'm pretty sure Victor said that."

"You were lead singer of the Road Rebels. I heard you guys play a few years ago at the Pavilion."

"That's me. Band split up about a year and half ago and I've been trying to get my solo career off the ground since then. This business is a bitch. Well, I'll see you opening night. Hope you're okay with runner-up to my first place."

Hunter didn't admit he'd be thrilled with that outcome, because number one, it would mean he'd made it to the finale, and number two, there would be no shame in losing to Rory Summit. The woman was an incredible guitarist and her vocal range was out of this world. He'd heard a rumor once that she'd actually trained with a retired opera singer all during high school.

Even so, he wasn't one to throw down the chance for some friendly trash-talking. "Flip that outcome and you'll have it right."

She laughed, then waved at Ailis. "Nice meeting you. Started out in this business because I was inspired by your parents and their music."

"Thanks," Ailis said, grinning widely. It wasn't unusual for people to say nice things about Sky and Teagan, but Ailis always looked as if the speaker had handed her a present. She was proud of her parents and their accomplishments.

Rory left and Hunter sighed. "What a night."

"I was about to say the same thing. This has certainly been an exciting time."

Hunter was surprised to see Ailis's Pop Pop standing there. He had seen him at the bar earlier, when he'd been auditioning, but the old guy was over ninety and not usually out this late.

"What are you still doing here, Pop Pop?" Ailis asked.

Mr. Collins shrugged. "I wasn't tired, and it's been some time since this place has felt so alive. Wasn't in a hurry to leave." He glanced toward the restaurant. "Even so, I expect Riley will come drag me out of here soon enough."

Then, the old man looked at him. "That was quite a show. I really enjoyed it."

Hunter sort of wondered if he meant the music or the fight. Mr. Collins was the type to probably get a kick out of both. "Thanks."

"I think you'll do well in that contest, son. Just listen to what our pretty little Ailis tells you to do and you'll win the whole damn thing."

"Pop Pop," Ailis said, blushing. "Hunter is the one competing, the one with the talent. I'm sure he'll—"

"I plan on doing everything she says. I'm nobody's fool. You don't have to worry about that, sir."

Mr. Collins's smile grew wide and he reached over to place a firm hand on Hunter's shoulder. "I knew you were a smart lad. Good for you."

"Hey, Pop, have you had enough yet?" Riley asked, walking over to join them. From the tone in her voice, it was obvious she'd tried to drag the old guy home several times already.

"Now," Mr. Collins said, "I'm ready. And just for the record, if I'd let you talk me into leaving earlier, I would have missed that fight."

Riley rolled her eyes. "And I'd never have heard the end of it. Must be some lucky star shining on me tonight." Her tone was pure Riley, which meant complete sarcasm. "Who was the dark-haired girl who just left?"

"Rory Summit," Hunter replied. "One of the competitors. She's seriously talented."

"And fucking hot," Riley added.

"Language, Riley," Mr. Collins said, chastising his adult daughter like she was some naughty teen.

"Sorry, Pop."

They all laughed as they said their goodbyes to Ailis's aunt and grandfather.

Ailis looked up at him. "Sorry about Pop Pop. When it comes to his grandchildren, he's convinced we've hung all the stars and the moon."

"He loves you. There's nothing wrong with that. And I meant what I said, I plan on doing everything you say."

"Even if it requires another *Pretty Woman*-style shopping excursion?"

Hunter feigned a wince. "I'll try to grin and bear it."

He thought she'd laugh, but her expression turned serious.

"What's wrong, mouse?"

"Nothing. I mean, I'm just thinking about that Victor guy and what he said and—"

"Les is going to hear about this, isn't he?"

She blew out a frustrated breath. "Yep."

"You think he'll kick me out of the show when he hears about that punch I just threw."

"Not if I have anything to say about it and definitely not after he finds out what the fucker said," Ailis said determinedly.

Hunter tucked his finger under her chin, tilting her face up to look at him. "Fighting my battles for me, mouse?"

"I don't need to do anything except clear a path for you to that stage. You're going to beat those assholes and win the whole damn thing."

Hunter chuckled. "I think I'm going to have to stop calling you mouse. You're my fierce warrior queen," he murmured.

Her gaze sharpened. "Hunter," she said warningly.

He blew out a long, frustrated breath.

"Ailis," he started, wishing he could figure out what it was that suddenly had him acting like a dog in heat whenever she was around. "I've never mastered self-control."

She narrowed her eyes as she studied his face. "Maybe not, but at some point, you have to see reason. Everything about this is wrong. You. Me. The timing. The situation."

"You're right," he agreed. "I know that."

She smirked. "Do you mind repeating the first part of that?"

Hunter tilted his head and crossed his arms. "Yeah, I do."

"You said I was right," she repeated for him.

"I get that the timing is bad for this..." Jesus, he couldn't begin to put a word to what he was feeling for her.

"Flirtation," she provided.

That was completely wrong, but Hunter decided to fly with it because her definition was way tamer and way more innocent than the vocabulary floating through his brain. "Yeah. Victor probably won't be the only one to think I'm getting some sort of free pass if people believe you and I are..." He really shouldn't have started this conversation.

"Having sex," she added.

He really wished she wouldn't say sex around him. It was a trigger. His cock thickened as he suddenly recalled Ailis's body quivering beneath his as she came. She'd been so tight and wet and hot, and his dick was having a hard time concentrating on anything other than the fact it hadn't been invited inside for a visit.

"So we have to put the brakes on all this kissing and," she continued, waving her hand around, "other stuff. I was serious about swearing off relationships. Until I get my head screwed on straight, I'm no good for anyone. Besides, you and I would never work anyway."

She kept saying that, but for the life of him right now—apart from the issue of timing—he couldn't figure out why she thought there were other obstacles in their way. "Why not?"

"Because we aren't heading in the same direction."

That really didn't make sense. Because for the first time in their lives, it appeared to him that they were both walking the same path side by side. He'd finally had a break in his career and, while she might not realize it, she'd had the same break in hers. "We're going in the exact same direction, Ailis."

"I need to keep my personal life simple right now. Preparing you so you can win the contest is going to take up every waking moment for the next few weeks. We can't lose focus. Eyes on the prize and all that."

"Good pep talk, coach."

She smiled, wrongly believing she'd convinced him with that silly argument of hers. "Then, when you win, you'll be on your way. Agents and recording studios will be clamoring to sign you. Legitimate agents," she stressed. "Ones with experience and connections. And," she paused, hesitating, "then you'll have everything you ever wanted. The career, the tour bus, the adoring fans, the fame."

"And you'll be right beside me, managing my career, beating off the groupies."

In typical fashion, she dodged the heart of his statement, seeking to make a joke instead. "You want the groupies run off?"

Hunter did, but saying that right now would spook her even more. "We'll work out signals in terms of the keepers and the ones getting tossed back."

"Wow. Comparing women to fish. So sexy and sweet. Why am I begging you to keep your hands off me again?"

In his sick mind, her sarcasm was probably one of the hottest things about her. "I have no idea why you won't let me touch you. You clearly loved my fingers inside you the other night," he whispered.

She closed her eyes, failing miserably at hiding how much she'd liked it too. When she finally looked at him again, her gaze was steadier. "I don't think we should discuss that again. You weren't there, remember?"

She damned him with his own words, so he changed the subject. "You act as if my success is a foregone conclusion. My chances of winning that contest aren't great. And even if I do, it's not as if it's my ticket to instant rock stardom. It's just a door opening."

"Do you know how frustrating it is that you can't see what I do?"

No one in his entire life had ever had so much faith in him. It was touching.

Then he considered her complaint. "Yeah, actually, I do know. Because I see the future *you're* meant to have in music too, A. And you keep walking away from it."

"Okay. You're right. I get it."

"Do you mind repeating that first part?" he teased.

"Yeah. I do." Then she turned to look at the door to her apartment longingly. "It's been a long night. I think I'm going to go up to bed."

"Alone?"

"Hunter," she warned.

"Fine. I'll see you tomorrow?"

She nodded. "We need to start preparing as soon as possible. I'll text you in the morning and we can figure out a time and place to meet."

"Sounds cool."

"Night," she said, as she turned and walked away.

Being reasonable sucked. Because even now, even after all her arguments and excuses, he wanted nothing more than to chase her to steal a good night kiss.

Then he'd stick around so he could steal a good morning one too.

Chapter Six

"Okay. Hold on a second," she yelled across the vast expanse of the room. Ailis skirted past the rows of chairs set up, walking straight toward the back of the room. Hunter was waiting on the stage for her to take her place.

For the entire month, they'd managed to hold firm to their return to "friends only" status.

However, the new norm felt like a farce. An act. They'd opened the lid to Pandora's box, and there was no putting that sucker back on again. She knew what it was like to kiss him, to have him touch her intimately, to feel the warmth in his eyes whenever he looked at her as if she was beautiful.

One minute, she and Hunter had been just going about their merry way, trying to get their lives on track. The next, he'd had his fingers buried deep inside her, and now she couldn't stop feeling things she didn't want to feel.

She couldn't fall in love with Hunter. She wouldn't.

But not for the reasons she'd told him.

Ailis had played the fool for love before. Been a very stupid smart girl, settling for things that didn't really make her happy. Hovering in the background while Paul's dreams came true. And she did all that with a man she'd believed to be honorable, steady, stable, safe.

Hunter was the opposite of that. He was impulsive, adventurous, and about to take the world by storm. If she hadn't believed that before—which she had—this past month had proven it to her beyond a doubt.

He'd worked his ass off. When he wasn't working at the inn, the two of them were together. The competition consisted of putting the contestants through a series of challenges, including their takes on a mix of hits from other musicians, as well as original works and instrumental solos. None of the artists knew what songs they were going to cover, so Ailis had assigned Hunter a different music genre each week, insisting that he familiarize himself with a wide array of numbers in that genre.

He was actually at an advantage with his background as a pub singer, because his repertoire was already quite vast. He could switch from country to rock to folk without blinking an eye. But his R&B was rusty, as was his heavy metal. And they needed to be ready for anything. God only knew what Les intended to throw at the performers.

The second Hunter was selected to compete, and Les had assigned her to represent him, she'd been removed from all aspects of planning the competition.

Les had reacted to the "fight" at the pub the way Hunter had feared. His first instinct had been to yank Hunter from the show. Until Ailis told him what Victor had said. Then he went quiet, introspective.

She didn't mistake the flash of anger in the older man's eyes that proved there would be a day of reckoning for Victor after the competition. However, he'd relented, allowing Hunter to remain in the contest.

As she'd thought, Les was pleased with the way his original plan was twisted in a way that served his purposes even better. He liked having her manage Hunter, determined it was a better trial run for her in terms of following what he still insisted was her destiny. Even so, just two days after Hunter had been selected to compete, Les had pulled all the performers and their managers into a meeting, where he explained the voting procedure in great detail—including how the winner would be selected by votes from the audience, and that management, including Sky and Teagan, had no control of the outcome.

Les then asked for questions, determined to clear the air. When Victor's agent pointed to Hunter and Ailis, Les assured everyone that Hunter was going to have to pull his weight on the stage to sway the crowd, and that he had no advantage simply because Sky and Teagan's daughter was managing him. Leah then made a snide comment about Hunter being her boyfriend. Les shut her down pretty fast, assuring her that no one's personal life meant a damn thing in the competition and she'd be smarter to focus on her performance.

Ailis appreciated Les's efforts on their behalf and she'd been determined not to let him down. He'd given her yet another good reason to push Hunter away. She didn't want to lose focus on her own performance—managing Hunter in such a way that he didn't embarrass himself or the competition. Les had put a lot of faith in her and she wanted to make sure she made him proud.

It had also helped that she and Hunter had been in nonstop motion since his audition. They'd bought at least a half a dozen different outfits for the first show—and God willing, the second—because Ailis wanted to see which of the looks they'd gone with worked best with the audience, particularly the females.

In addition to rehearsing potential covers, she'd spent some time with him, tweaking the wording, as well as the actual tunes, to some of his strongest original works. She was by no means a musician, but she'd been around singers and songwriters her whole life. As such, she was familiar with what words evoked stronger emotions for listeners, and she appreciated the subtle science of slowing down or speeding up a melody to draw out the perfect effect.

Then she'd coached him prior to the three interviews Les had set up for each performer. Les was determined to have a full house for all four shows, so he'd arranged for radio and local news stations to interview the eight contestants to help build the excitement. She wasn't sure if Les had told the reporters that her role as Hunter's manager was off-the-record or if the journalists didn't know who she was, but mercifully, none of them had questioned him about her.

Through it all, Hunter had taken every piece of her advice, soaking up every drop of her guidance like a sponge. She'd been pleasantly surprised by his earnestness to learn, expecting to have to fight to convince him that some things needed to be planned, not improvised.

That fight never happened.

"How far away are you going?" Hunter asked into the microphone.

"You have to play to the entire audience, Hunter," she yelled. The room was huge. "You have to be able to project yourself effectively to the back as well as the front."

"I feel like I should be able to make that into a crude joke, but I'm struggling in this space. I don't think I realized…"

His words faded away and she was glad they had this opportunity, no matter how brief, to feel out the arena. The competition started tonight, and as such, Les had made arrangements for each performer to spend forty-five minutes on the stage to test out their instruments and to get familiar with the setup. While that would probably be enough for the others who had played on countless stages, Hunter needed the time to become accustomed to playing in such a large space. The Baltimore Soundstage was a far cry from Pat's Pub.

"Okay," she called out. "Go ahead and start your first number. Remember, you need to make every single fan in the audience feel as if you're singing to them, as well as the ones watching on their computers at home. You can't focus on the first three rows just because those are the only faces you can see. Focus on the cameras part of the time and even though I'm way back here in no-man's-land, I've paid my money to come listen to you as well, and I get a vote too. So grab it."

Hunter strummed the first few chords of his guitar. They'd checked the sound prior to her journey away from the stage. It sounded great.

He started singing an upbeat number. She watched him for a few moments before calling out his name.

"Hey! Hunter!"

He stopped playing. "What's wrong?"

"You need to fill the space."

"What?"

She gestured to the stage. "It's a large area, and you aren't moving. We've rigged you up with that wireless headset mic so that you can walk around. Work the stage!"

"I feel like a goddamn marching band."

She laughed. "Don't march. Just take a casual stroll back and forth with some meaningful pauses. You'll get the hang of it."

He resumed playing, and, though it took him a couple of trips across the stage before he loosened up, eventually he made it look somewhat natural.

Once again, she was impressed by how willing he was to listen, as well as how quickly he picked things up. She'd said it a million times in the past few weeks, and she meant it. He was a born entertainer.

He was handsome in a rugged, just-rolled-out-of-bed-after-fucking-you-senseless way. Women were going to fall in love with him. Hell, he already had a fair number of groupies at the pub. She could only begin to imagine how that number would swell after this performance. Every woman in Baltimore would be tossing her panties onto that stage.

Which was why she needed to shed these unwanted feelings of lust as soon as possible. While he might think he wanted her at the moment, that was going to change the second he saw how much his playing field was about to grow.

She tried to ignore the pierce of jealousy that flashed when she considered all the beautiful women he'd encounter once he started touring. Ailis had witnessed countless groupies throwing themselves at her father, even though they knew he was happily married and his wife and children were right there. She never ceased to be amazed by the outright audacity and tenacity of some of the women.

She had asked her mom once how she could stand it. As always, her mom's response was simple and from the heart. She said it didn't bother her because she and Dad had two things that even the most beautiful woman in the world couldn't destroy. Love and trust.

Love and trust.

Ailis had spent her entire life longing for those things, but after Paul, she wasn't able to trust herself when it came to finding love. Her battered heart was scared and her pride wouldn't let her trust easily.

Fool me once, shame on Paul.

But fool me twice and the fault will be all mine.

Then she recalled Hunter's comments at New Year's. He'd asked her to trust him. And for a very brief moment, she had. And he hadn't abused it. Hadn't hurt her.

But that didn't mean she could offer him more. There was a big difference between thirty minutes and a lifetime.

The song came to an end and Ailis silently chastised herself for letting her thoughts drift instead of paying attention. Hunter was counting on her to guide him. She couldn't keep wallowing in self-doubt.

"Well?" he asked when she didn't speak.

"You're getting it. That sounded amazing."

"Really? Because I feel super self-conscious up here."

She started walking back to the stage so she didn't have to keep yelling. "I thought you liked being the center of attention."

He grinned. "Very funny. You sure that walking around didn't look...stiff?"

Once she reached the stage, she looked up as he approached her, reaching down to half drag, half lift her until she stood next to him. He took the headset off and placed it next to his guitar stand.

"I think you just need to work out a pattern. Like this." The two of them meandered to the left, pausing for several beats before strolling to the far right. "Let your music decide when you move and how fast. If it's easier to walk when you're just playing and not singing, let that be your cue to move."

"I actually think it's easier when I'm singing."

"Then go with that. Pick a person's face near the front as your guide and just sort of walk to them as you sing. If you choose a pretty girl and you flash that damn lethal smile, her panties will melt away and she'll start declaring her undying love for you."

"Is that right?" he asked, shooting her the exact grin she'd just described. "So where are you going to be standing tonight? I might give that a try."

It was the first time in a month he'd said anything even relatively sexual to her. She thought they'd turned this corner.

"Hunter—"

He placed his guitar in the stand and stepped behind her. She offered no resistance when his chest pressed against her back and his hands found their way around her waist. Her head wasn't finished waging the battle, but her body had been feeling the serious effects of deprivation. It was winning at the moment. Especially when his fingers drifted beneath her shirt, coming to rest on the waistband on her jeans.

"Could I make your panties melt away?"

"Hunter—" she repeated.

"Don't run through that same old grocery list of excuses either, mouse. I've got the damn thing memorized. Just think about the question and answer it honestly."

"Yes," she said without hesitation.

Her quick response clearly shocked him. But he recovered fast. His lips hovered by her ear as he whispered, "If I dipped my fingers inside these jeans, would your panties be wet right now?"

She nodded.

For a second, she thought he was going to test that theory. Her hands flew up to grip his wrists to stop him.

"There are people all over this place setting up for tonight."

"They're busy. They're not looking at us."

He seemed to be speaking the truth. The place was a hive of activity as everyone worked double time to complete preparations for the show.

"Come home with me after the show tonight."

Ailis twisted in his arms, trying to put some space between them. It didn't work. Hunter held fast. "Why won't you—"

He kissed her. Goddammit. She was not this woman. She didn't let a guy manhandle her or shut her up with sexy-as-fuck kisses every time she was about to say something he didn't want to hear.

Except she did with him.

Her hands were around his neck and her tongue was in his mouth in an instant. The last month had been pure torture. He'd turned something on inside her over New Year's and she couldn't find the switch to turn it off again.

His hands lingered beneath her shirt, his thumbs caressing the sensitive skin of her waist. She hadn't lied about the current state of affairs in her panties. Primarily because she'd been dealing with wet panties for a fair amount of January. There was something about the scent of Hunter's shampoo combined with his voice as he sang or when he laughed. God, everything he did turned her on, fired her libido up until it was unbearable to be with him and not touch him.

The kiss would have lasted a lot longer if not for Rory.

"Hey. Hate to interrupt because that was a hot fucking kiss, and given my current dry spell, living vicariously through you two is sort of giving me urges I thought were gone forever, but it's my turn to practice."

"Does that mean you're not dating Eddie Keene anymore?" Hunter asked.

Rory shook her head sadly. "It's never smart to date your lead guitarist. When we fell apart, so did the band."

"I'm sorry, Rory. About Eddie. And um, you know," Ailis said, hating how hot her cheeks were. PDA wasn't something she had much—okay, any—experience with.

Apparently being a natural redhead meant that every other part of her felt the need to follow suit. Her chronic blushing was the bane of her existence. It always made her feel as though she was that same shy four-year-old hiding behind her mother.

"No problem. You two make a cute couple. Look, I hate to rush you, but I want to make sure I grab as much stage time as possible so I can get out of here before Victor shows up. Prick always tries to offer me advice. As if I'd listen to anything his talentless ass has to offer. Twenty bucks says he's out tonight."

Ailis considered taking Rory up on the bet. Not because she had strong feelings one way or the other, but because she'd clearly been hanging around her family too long. There was something in the Collins's genes that made it impossible for them to resist a bet.

She smiled to herself when she realized how strong the pull actually was. And here she was, thinking she didn't fit in with her crazy family. She liked discovering she was wrong.

"Down girl," Hunter joked, looking at Ailis. "Your Collins's colors are shining through. Pretty sure Les would kick your ass if you started wagering on the outcome. Even if it would be nice to see Victor voted out tonight."

Ailis grimaced. "Les seems to think Victor has a decent shot at winning."

Mari Carr

Rory shrugged, clearly not concerned with the competition. "We'll see. My gut says he's going to choke. Big time."

"Hope you're right. We're done," Hunter said, unplugging his guitar. "Be out of your way in a jiffy."

"No worries." Rory started setting up as Ailis caught sight of Les backstage. He was staring directly at her, looking pensive. There was no doubt in her mind Rory hadn't been the only witness to that kiss. When he caught her looking at him, he turned and walked away.

Great. How could she have been so stupid? This wasn't going to end well.

"I'll meet you at the car, Hunter," Ailis said. "There's something I need to take care of really quick."

She took off in the direction Les had gone, catching him near one of the dressing rooms.

"Hey, Les. I wanted to..." She stumbled at the scowl on his face.

"You and the pub singer an item?"

She shook her head, trying to quickly deny it. "No. That was just, um..." So much for being an intelligent woman. Every vocabulary word she'd ever known flew out of her head.

Les narrowed his eyes. "You've never lied to me before, kiddo. I'd hate to see you break that streak."

"We're not a thing," she insisted a little too loudly. "I mean...I think he might want us to be, um, I don't know, something." She wasn't going to say "fling" because that would send Les into orbit. He was as overprotective of her as her dad, uncles, cousins and grandfather. Jesus. No woman should have that many alpha male relatives in one family. "But I..."

"You what?"

"The timing isn't right. I mean, he's got the show tonight and he needs to concentrate on that. And then there's the chance that this contest might lead to bigger

and better things for him. If it does and his career takes
off, he'll be heading out on the road, touring. And that's
not to mention the fact we're a complete mismatch.
He's a show-off, a charmer. I've always seen myself
with a quieter man, someone happy to sit on the back
porch and read with me, or watch indie films, or go to
wineries to do tastings, or..."

"Damn. That's a lot of excuses. You had all those
at the ready, didn't you?"

She frowned. "They aren't excuses."

"Of course they are. But tell me, Ailis, who are you
trying to convince? You or me?"

"You always say never get involved with the
talent."

He nodded. "That's right. I do. And believe me,
before you launched into all that bullshit, that was
exactly what was on the tip of my tongue to say."

"So why don't you?"

"Because I'm not about to give you another lame
excuse."

She bit her lower lip, not wanting to get into a fight
with Les. She loved the man, respected him and his
opinion. But he was wrong about this. She'd given a lot
of thought to her and Hunter as a couple these past few
weeks, and she couldn't shake the feeling that anything
between them would be destined to fail. She wasn't
sure she was strong enough yet. Strong enough to fall in
love, to trust a man...hell, to trust herself not to get lost
again.

"I think you should tell me not to get involved,"
she said, hating the pleading in her voice.

"No. You've been hiding backstage for most of
your life, Ailis. It's time for you to step out of the
shadows and claim your spotlight."

"I hope that's an analogy, because there's no way
in hell I'll ever step on a stage—"

"Don't play dumb with me, girl."

"Fine. I get it. Stop hiding at the pub. Stop waitressing. Stop wasting my life." All the things she'd had to listen to for the past year came spilling out of her hotly. "I love how everyone tells me over and over what I'm doing wrong, acting as if it should be the simplest thing in the world to fix all the shit. It's not that easy, Les."

He sighed, his eyes softening, making her feel like crap for her outburst. "It's the simplest thing on earth, kiddo. You're pretty good at fixating on the negatives. Maybe open your ears and listen to the positives. There are lots of people who love you who are showing you the way. More than that, they're willing to help you get there. But you have to stop questioning everyone's motives and doubting yourself."

"I don't..." She couldn't finish the lie. Couldn't say something that wasn't true.

"If you wiped away all those stupid excuses about the pub singer, how would you feel about him?"

"I—" *love him.* She couldn't say that aloud, couldn't admit it. Not to Les, not to Hunter. Not even to herself. Because love fucked a person up. She'd loved Paul. Honestly. Sincerely. He'd ripped her heart out. He'd stomped all over her trust. They'd started out as just friends too and then she'd let them be something more. And that's when she disappeared. Ailis stopped existing as her own person and Paul took over, deciding where they should live, talking her into that job at the marketing firm because her original career plan of managing tours would take her away from him too much. If Hunter won the competition, the same thing would happen. She'd start playing follow the leader again, going where he went, letting his life decide hers. She couldn't do that anymore.

"It's okay, kiddo. You don't have to answer. I can see the truth in your eyes even if you can't. I can also see the panic setting in. Take a deep breath and step away from it for a little while. Because you're right. You and Hunter need to concentrate on tonight's show. Get through that. The rest of this will sit a bit."

"Nothing can come of it."

"Yeah. We'll see about that."

"I'm not going to lose my head again. I promise."

Les sighed. "I didn't ask for that promise. Go ahead and keep kissing the boy. It's good for you."

What was going on with the men in her life? Les was every bit as overprotective as Padraig. Yet both of them looked the other way when it came to Hunter.

"Les—"

"Got a lot to do, kiddo. I'll see you tonight at the show." He didn't say anything else. Instead, Les walked away and left her standing there staring at an empty hallway.

Hunter was waiting for her at the car by now. Part of her wanted to run the opposite direction. Her emotions were riding too close to the surface. Facing him would be too damn hard.

He wanted things from her that she couldn't give. Could she?

She walked to the car, feeling numb, confused, frustrated.

Reckless.

Ailis opened the passenger door and climbed in.

"Want me to drop you off at your place to get ready for the show? I can pick you up in a few hours."

She shook her head. "No. I want you to take me back to your place."

Hunter ran a hand through his hair. "I think I need a break, A. I'm pretty sure there's nothing we could do now that would help me be any more prepared."

"I don't want to practice. I want you."

"What the hell are you talking about?"

Ailis ignored the flames licking her face and powered through. "Sex."

He frowned, and his reaction caught her off guard. Had she misread everything that had been happening between them? Even though he'd adhered to a mostly hands-off policy lately, always being on his best behavior, she'd caught glimpses of the way he looked at her. While she was no expert on the subject, she was pretty sure his expressions reflected lust. And then there was that invitation on the stage.

When he didn't say anything, she reached for the door handle, desperate for escape.

Hunter threw the lock on the door from his side. "Now you want to have sex with me."

Ailis wasn't sure if an answer was required because he hadn't really asked a question. "I think I must have misunderstood—"

"You didn't misunderstand a damn thing. I want you too. So badly it hurts. You have any idea how hard it is to walk around with a hard-on in your pants day after day?"

"I've been hurting too."

"I jack off every single day after you leave. I close my eyes and imagine those bright blue eyes looking at me. That silky red hair wrapped around my fingers. Your soft, full lips on my mouth, on my dick. I'm obsessed with you, Ailis. You consume every second of my day and then you sneak into my damn dreams when I'm asleep."

He got it. He did understand. They were both driving themselves mad, longing for something they thought they couldn't have. She'd told him she needed love with sex. But the truth was, she didn't. They were both adults, attracted to each other. They had a genuine fondness for each other.

"So you agree it's a good idea. We'll go back to your place. We'll do it, and then all these pent-up desires will go away and we can get on with our lives as normal."

Hunter tilted his head. "You want a one-night stand?"

She glanced outside at the brightly shining sun. "I think in our case, it would be a one-afternoon stand."

He shook his head. "No."

It took Ailis a minute to figure out what he was talking about. He wanted this. He'd just admitted to it. "No?"

"It won't be one time."

Hunter was the king of one-night stands. She'd been his confidante for a solid year, and she knew for a fact he hadn't taken the same woman to bed more than once in all that time.

"Of course it will."

He crossed his arms, refusing to start the car, to put them on the road back to his place where they could blow off all this damn steam.

"No, mouse. If you go home with me this afternoon, it's with the knowledge that we're going to do this thing right."

"I have no idea what that means." She'd actually decided on the walk to the car that this afternoon was the perfect day to do this, because their time was finite. They couldn't linger in bed afterwards because they had to get ready for the show.

"Okay. Tell you what. When you figure it out and agree, I'll take you to my bed. Until then..."

He wasn't going to accept her offer. "Until then?"

"We burn."

She closed her eyes, trying to fight back the tears forming. "I can't do this anymore, Hunter."

"I know, baby. But I can't do a one-time thing with you. I just can't."

She was tired of being rejected. What the hell was wrong with her? Paul didn't want to marry her. Hunter didn't want to fuck her. "Great. Damned if I do, damned if I don't. You only want me until I want *you*, and then—"

"Stop it, Ailis."

She looked at him. "Stop what?"

"Stop acting like there's something wrong with you. Paul was a tool who didn't know what he had. He fucked up, choosing Rhonda over you. That's not on you. It's on him."

"So what's your excuse?" she spat out angrily.

"I'm not a fool. I know exactly what I could have with you. You want sex. That's awesome. More than awesome. But I'm not going to rush into something just because you want to scratch an itch. When we sleep together, it's going to be for the right reasons—and there won't be any regrets."

"I won't regret it."

He cupped her cheek. "Says the woman who spent the last year swearing off sex without love. And then the last two months swearing off love."

"It's not like I'm a virgin, Hunter. You said it yourself. Sex and love don't have to be connected."

He grinned. "Not sure I've ever seen you so freaked out. You're always so steady, so logical."

She frowned. "I'm not freaked out." Her argument might have been more convincing if she hadn't screeched it at him.

"You're scared to death."

Ailis threw her hands up in frustration. "Of what?"

"Everything."

She didn't have an answer to that. Because in this moment, she was completely terrified.

Of everything.

"Please don't say no," she whispered. "Guys like girls who put out on the first date, remember?" She hoped her joke would alleviate some of the tension pulsing in the air, making her heart race, her chest tight.

He pressed his forehead against hers. "You're my best friend, mouse. One of the best I've ever had."

"That's not much of a compliment, considering your other bestie was Paul."

He kissed her quickly. "You're turning into a regular smart-ass these days."

"Whose fault is that?"

Hunter didn't reply. Instead, he leaned back in his seat, facing the windshield. He made no move to start the car.

"What's wrong?" she asked.

"I'm trying to force myself to drive you back to your place."

"First time I try to be impulsive and you shoot me down."

He looked at her through narrowed eyes. "You're not helping."

She gave him the sexiest smile she could manage. "Wasn't trying to."

Hunter reached over and mussed up her hair, something he did on a fairly regular basis because he knew it drove her nuts. She batted his hand away.

"Take me home, you idiot. Maybe I can find some hot stranger at the pub to be spontaneous with."

The look he shot her was pure male possession that sent a lightning strike of arousal straight to her pussy.

She put her hands up in instant surrender. "Kidding. Just kidding."

"You better be," he muttered, as he started the car.

The drive back to the pub was made in silence, which was a relief as much as it unnerved her. She couldn't figure out what the hell had just happened. In the course of an hour, she'd lost her freaking mind.

When he pulled into a parking space in front of the pub, he put the car in park but didn't turn off the engine.

She didn't get out. Instead, she kept her gaze straight ahead, looking down the cobblestone street.

"You invited me back to your place tonight after the show," she said after a few awkward silent minutes.

"I did, but, Ailis—"

"But you don't want a one-night stand."

"No. I don't."

"This would all be a lot easier if—"

"I'm not going to argue about that again, mouse. Just take the afternoon and think about it. Okay?"

"Okay." She reached over to open her door.

Hunter grabbed her hand and winked at her, the picture of confidence, even though she knew he was nervous about tonight. "See you in a few hours."

She suddenly hated herself for pulling this act of insanity on him just a few hours before what was likely one of the biggest nights of his life. She was an idiot. "You've got this, Hunter."

He shook his head. "*We've* got this."

She got out of the car, trying to ignore how good it felt to be included in a "we" after so long as a "me."

Chapter Seven

"As you know, ladies and gentleman, two of our eight performers will be returning home tonight based on your votes. The accounting firm of Blake, Vale and Ogle is doing one last check of the results, and as soon as we have them— Wait. Wait just a moment."

Hunter stood under the hot lights and wondered what was going to kill him first. The rapid-fire beat of his heart growing faster and faster until it exploded, or the stroke looming thanks to his sky-high blood pressure. Or maybe he'd just spontaneously combust on this stuffy, airless stage.

He glanced backstage and was only mildly mollified by the fact Ailis looked just as nervous as he felt. Her porcelain skin was paler than normal, and she was destroying the ends of the scarf she'd worn to the show, wringing the material so tightly there wasn't an iron on earth that would flatten it again.

He'd stumbled a bit during his first number, fucking up some of the lyrics, overwhelmed by the sheer number of people in the crowd. However, he'd found his sweet spot by the second song, and he'd played off the energy in the room. The folks there had come for a good show and he had to admit, he felt like all of the performers had given it to them.

Even so, he'd been intimidated. A big audience for him was a busy night at the pub, which meant no more than fifty or sixty people. Ailis told him they'd sold nearly every ticket for the first night's show, and Les anticipated the attendance would only continue to grow with each subsequent week as word of mouth brought more fans and the regulars returned to support their favorites. Hunter had already overheard some talk while he was waiting backstage for his turn to perform of moving the finale to an even larger venue, something Les had planned for in case the show took off the way he'd hoped.

God only knew how many people were watching this thing live over the internet. He glanced toward the cameras pointed toward him. He'd had to force himself to look at them several times during his performance, trying not to think about the fact there could be hundreds, thousands, sweet Jesus, millions of unseen people watching him.

The voting was done by a special app attendees and viewers downloaded to their phones.

"Alright," the announcer said. "How exciting is this? To build the anticipation, we're starting at the top and working our way down the field. So, who is safe and definitely returning next week? If each performer would step over here," he gestured to the right of the stage, which was currently empty except for the six X's someone had taped to the floor to mark the spot where the finalists should stand, "when their name is called."

Hunter prayed he'd find himself on that side of the stage. The night of the audition, all he had considered was how huge this could be for his career, but as this past month progressed, he realized he wanted this as much for Ailis as himself. She didn't seem to realize her innate talent as a manager. She'd worked every bit as hard as he had, and he didn't want to let her down.

"In first place—and the competitor who is definitely returning next week—is Rory Summit!"

Rory had legitimately killed it during her performance. There wasn't a person in the entire place surprised by her win.

Hunter stood stone-still, no longer breathing as the announcer moved Leah, Robbie and a talented pianist named Wes to the right side of the stage. They were all safe and coming back next week. Half the field was gone and Hunter was starting to lose hope. Not that he had expected to be top of the list.

"And the fifth-place performer who will be returning next week is Baltimore's very own local pub singer, Hunter Maxwell!"

Hunter somehow managed to cross the stage on wooden legs. He made it. He'd advanced to the second week.

As soon as he found his way to his X, he looked backstage, wanting to find Ailis, wanting to see her face.

She didn't disappoint him. She was in the midst of hugging everyone within arm's reach, and he wasn't sure, but he thought he saw her grab Les and tug his head down to kiss the top of the older man's bald pate.

He chuckled at the sight, causing Rory to look over and wink at him.

When he glanced back, Ailis had finally calmed down enough to return her attention to the stage, to him. He'd never seen her smile so big, so genuine. His heart jumped and thudded harder than it had been just a few minutes earlier.

Sweet Jesus. What the hell had happened to her?

No. Wrong question. The more accurate one was what the fuck was wrong with *him*?

How had he missed this? Missed that beauty? That light that seemed to shine out of every part of her for so long?

It was as if the veil she'd hidden behind had finally fallen completely away, and now it took every ounce of strength he possessed not to run to her or pass out under the lights from the ever-increasing temperature in his body.

The announcer, Mike O'Shea, a local newscaster, added the last name to the list—Jenni St. James—which left Victor and another woman, Belle French, on the wrong side of the stage.

Hunter stopped listening to Mike's chatter about it being a great competition and inviting them to return next week. Instead, he focused on a very bitter, very angry Victor as he stormed off the stage. When he passed Ailis, he turned and said something to her. Something that wiped the gorgeous smile off her face. Ailis frowned, and Hunter struggled to decide if she was angry or scared. He was too far away to tell.

He silently willed Mike to wrap it up, but the man was clearly enjoying his role as master of ceremonies. Finally, after another five minutes, he bid everyone a good night, and Hunter was free to walk over to Ailis.

It was on the tip of his tongue to demand to know what Victor had said to her. That bastard was cruising for another helping of his fist, but before he could open his mouth, Ailis was in his arms.

"You were fifth," she cried out in delight. "Fifth!"

"That won't be good enough next week," he said.

She gripped him tighter. "Shut up. Don't kill my happy buzz!"

He laughed. "Wouldn't think of it. What did Victor say?"

"Accused me and Les of colluding together. He thinks we got one of the sound guys to tamper with his earpiece to pay him back for that scene at the pub. Said he couldn't hear the music. I have to admit, I believe him. He was really struggling to find his place."

"And he seriously thinks that's your fault?"

"He needed an outlet. I was the first person he saw." She hugged him again. "I'm so freaking happy right now!"

He laughed again and accepted her embrace.

Ailis was forced to release him when Les stepped over to shake his hand and congratulate him. "Good job, Hunter. I'll admit I had my reservations about how you'd manage in the contest, but I should have known better. Ailis knows talent when she sees it."

"My talent alone wouldn't have gotten me to the next round," Hunter said. "I wouldn't be in next week's show without Ailis's guidance, her knowledge. This was her win as much as mine."

"Mmph," Les grunted. "Keep saying shit like that, son, and I'm going to have to start liking you. And I like very few people."

Ailis laughed. "Oh hush, Les. What do you say we hit the pub to celebrate? I've already texted Tris and Padraig. Uncle Sean set it up so the competition played over all the big screens. Apparently, everyone is lining up at the bar to buy you a drink."

Hunter grinned. "That sounds like a plan."

The two of them headed to the car, and Hunter listened with great amusement as Ailis dissected his performance, from the second he walked out onto the stage until he walked off again. She had pointed out no less than twelve things they needed to work on for next week, and she'd changed her mind about some small part of the outfit they'd intended for him to wear during the second show. Her mind was going a mile a minute and she was sharing it all in rapid-fire commentary.

Hunter tried to follow along, to pay attention, but his eyes kept sneaking glimpses of her lips, her breasts.

"Your hair looks pretty tonight, A. I love it down like that."

She stumbled briefly, obviously confused by his completely off-topic compliment. "Thanks," she said. "I used the flat iron. I was also thinking about Rory's performance. I think there are a lot of things you could pick up from her that..." She kept talking, but Hunter's attention wavered again, recalling that kiss they'd shared on the stage earlier in the day.

"Hunter," she said, pointing. "There's a spot. Better grab it. Rare to get one this close to the pub."

He parked the car, then slid around the front of the hood quickly to help her out. He took her hand in his again, lifting it to kiss her knuckles. She gave him a happy grin.

"You might have to spend the night on the couch tonight if things get as out of control as I think they will. There's nothing the Irish like more than a celebration."

"The couch sounds good." Not as good as her bed, of course. He'd told her to think about his invitation this afternoon. Looked like Ailis wasn't finished fighting.

The atmosphere in Pat's Pub was just as Ailis had warned. The place was packed as everyone wanted to share in his success, and he was treated to more than a few congratulatory shots. He accepted one after another from the patrons, who'd always cheered him on night after night here at the pub. But he resisted drinking them all, finding ways to share them with Ailis and her cousins. He didn't want to get drunk tonight. He already felt tipsy, slightly off-balance just from looking at Ailis. Adding alcohol didn't seem like a good idea.

Ailis had opted for the alcohol version of tipsy, though she was also a far cry from drunk.

She was laughing at some joke Finn had told when his powers of resistance faltered. He leaned over and kissed her. Right in the middle of the pub. At a table with no less than six of her cousins.

Tris appeared beside him fairly quickly. Hunter would have laughed if not for the knowledge that he needed both hands unbroken to play the guitar.

"Thinking maybe you've had enough to drink tonight," Ailis's uncle said, though not with the usual amount of intimidation he might have used on a stranger who'd kissed one of his nieces. Obviously, Tris thought Hunter had drunk all the shots he'd delivered and was wasted and putting the moves on Ailis.

"Yeah," Hunter said, standing on very steady feet. "I *have* had enough."

His lack of slurred words had Tris studying him more closely. "You're not drunk," the older man said at last.

"Not even a little bit," Hunter assured him.

"But—"

"Uncle Tris," Ailis said, stumbling as she tried to stand next to Hunter. "It's just Hunter."

"Yeah, but—"

Ailis's Pop Pop stepped next to him. "I wonder if I might have a word with Hunter alone."

Shit. Hunter would have preferred to get his ass handed to him by Ailis's uncles. Disappointing Mr. Collins was something he never wanted to do.

"Sure thing, Pop," Tris said, returning to the bar.

Mr. Collins and Hunter both looked at Ailis, who hadn't moved.

"Why don't you run on upstairs, sweetheart? I'll send your young man up to say good night after our chat."

"He's not my—"

Hunter cut her off. "I'll be up in a few minutes, A."

Ailis was hesitant to leave, but when it was clear no conversation was going to happen until she did, she dragged herself away, disappearing through the doorway that led to her apartment.

"Mr. Collins—" Hunter began.

"Come grab a seat at the bar with me."

The two of them sat on the high stools. "You want a drink?" Mr. Collins, ever the barman, asked.

Hunter shook his head. "No. Believe me, I'm good. Had more than enough. Listen, Mr. Collins, if you're planning to warn me off, to tell me to stay away from Ailis—"

Mr. Collins frowned. "Stay away? From Ailis? Why, no, that's not my purpose at all. What I want to say is it's about time."

"Time?" Hunter tried to figure out where he'd missed a step...or three.

Mr. Collins rolled his eyes. "This is going to be a long talk if you don't try to keep up, son. It's about time you took off those blinders you've been wearing and realized what was standing right in front of you."

"Ailis?"

"I know the two of you got knocked down a peg when those blasted idiots ran off to Vegas. And it's taken some time for you and Ailis to lick your wounds. It appears you've healed faster."

"Healed?"

"Keep trying, son. You're almost there. I've been watching you tonight—actually, for the past few months. I've seen the way you look at Ailis. Not hard to recognize a man in love."

Hunter shook his head. "Love?"

Mr. Collins patted Hunter on the shoulder, a kind, fatherly sort of touch that was half support and half sympathy. There was no denying Mr. Collins was looking at him as if he was six eggs short of a dozen.

"I don't have it wrong. And you know it. Maybe you don't want to admit it to yourself yet, and that's okay. Like I said, there's been some heartbreak to recover from. Makes sense that you and Ailis would build a few protective walls. The trick is to not cower behind them forever. You're starting to peek out. I'm not sure Ailis is. So, I want to ask a favor of you."

Hunter nodded, simply because he couldn't think of anything to say. He was feeling overwhelmed and maybe even a little bit exposed. It had been a hell of a night.

"I want you to drag her out. She's always been a quiet little thing, spends a lot of time in her head, thinking. She's a smart girl, one who grew up surrounded by adults, rather than kids her own age, so I'm not sure she had a lot of experience with cutting loose and having fun until this year with you. The doctor used her—used her brains, her kindness, her seriousness. I think you and I both know she did the lion's share of his homework for him."

Hunter grimaced. Paul had admitted as much to him one night when they'd been three sheets to the wind. It wasn't that Paul wasn't intelligent enough to do the work himself. He was just lazy. "Yeah."

"She comes alive with you. She talks more these days. Laughs more."

Hunter hadn't realized that until Mr. Collins said it. He thought back to the Ailis, the mouse, who'd been his best friend's girlfriend. She'd rarely spoken, rarely smiled. It wasn't that she wasn't pleasant, she was just distant, content to hover in the corners of the room, watching the world go by. Maybe that was the beacon he was seeing lately.

"It's time for her to use those brains of hers for something other than waitressing. We were happy to take her in after Paul walked out because she needed us and we missed having her in our lives. We all rallied around because that's what family does. But we've made it too easy for her to stay."

Hunter considered everything Ailis had done for him today—the outfit, the music advice, the fans. "It's not just the waitressing. She was wasted at the marketing firm too."

Mr. Collins's smile grew. "That she was, but for a girl who grew up on the road, I think she spent a fair amount of time coveting what the rest of us had here."

"She says she doesn't want to go back out on the road."

"Well now, I think that was true for a while. The old adage holds steady here. The grass is always greener on the other side. You've only ever known the Ailis who lives in Baltimore. I knew the Ailis who was on the bus. She loved that lifestyle too, though she doesn't admit it. Lately, I've been thinking she even misses it."

Hunter thought he'd recognized a spark of wanderlust growing in her eyes whenever she talked about the possibility of him going out on tour. "I think so too."

"You're a talented young man. I've seen a lot of musicians in my time. You're the...what is it they say? The real deal. Ailis can help you get where you're going."

"Yeah," Hunter said. "Yeah, I think she can."

"But you can get her where she needs to go too. That's the difference between you and the doctor."

Mr. Collins had mentioned blinders. Hunter hadn't realized he'd been wearing them until that moment onstage...when they fell away.

His future had started tonight.

And so had hers.

He wondered how long it would have taken him to be able to admit the truth if not for her grandfather. "Mr. Collins—" he started.

"*Och.* No need to thank me, son. That's just wasting time you could spend with our girl. Go give her a kiss goodnight."

Hunter stood, unable to hide his smile. For the first time in forever, he wasn't going to fly by the seat of his pants. He had a plan, a solid one.

By the time he reached the door to Ailis's bedroom, he was more determined than ever. He glanced through the open doorway to find her pacing.

"What did Pop Pop want?"

Hunter knew she was going to ask him. And he wasn't about to tell her. "To congratulate me."

She raised one disbelieving eyebrow. "And he needed to do that in private?"

He reached out and stroked her hair affectionately. "You know, every now and then, you might just want to let me get away with something."

Ailis seemed to consider that, then said, "I might. But tonight isn't one of those times."

"Fine," Hunter said, cupping her cheeks in his palms. "He told me to kiss you goodnight."

"I highly doubt—"

That was as much as he heard before he did exactly as her grandfather suggested. A handful of kisses in and Hunter was completely addicted.

His tongue touched hers and she moved closer, her hands fisting his hair, tugging it, using it to hold him there. If his mouth had been free, he would have told her she didn't have to worry. He wasn't going anywhere. His hands drifted away from her face, sliding along her back.

"Caitlyn?" he murmured.

"Staying at Lucas's."

He figured as much. Caitlyn had all but moved in with the billionaire, though she didn't seem ready to admit the guy was her boyfriend. What was it with these Collins women that made them so resistant to commit? Then he recalled that—like Ailis—Caitlyn had suffered a pretty serious heartbreak as well.

So maybe the question was, what was wrong with the men in Baltimore?

"Good. Are you ready?" he asked.

"Ready?"

"For you and me, A, because this is happening."

She tilted her head, confused. "You're going to have to clarify what exactly is happening."

"Everything."

"Sex?"

He nodded.

"Okay. I want that too. Wait, are you drunk?"

"You know I'm not."

"Is this some sort of adrenaline rush? Horniness caused by elation?"

He laughed. "Do you want to have sex with me, Ailis, or not?"

She bit her lower lip and looked away as if trying to decide.

"You wanted it this afternoon. Have you reconsidered?"

She shook her head slowly as if searching for the right words. Ailis was a thinker, which meant it took her longer to speak, but when she did, he knew he was hearing the truth. "You said it's going to be more than one night."

"Actually, what I just said was *everything*."

"Define that."

He leaned closer. "You know exactly what that means."

"I'm not sure I do."

"You'll figure it out."

"Hunter, I think maybe we need to talk about—"

"No, we don't." He cut off anything else she might want to say with a hard kiss. Then he turned around and shut the door, throwing the lock. Her cousins were all still downstairs celebrating without them. Hopefully they'd stay there a while.

Her place wasn't ideal for what he had in mind. Her bed was too small, but there was no way they'd make it back to his apartment without getting arrested for public indecency. He needed her naked and under him now.

She waited until he came back to her before placing a hand on his chest to hold him back.

"You're not going to throw that 'I'm waiting for marriage' crap at me, are you?"

She shook her head. "I never said marriage. I said love. And I think we know that was a lie. It was a way to make me feel safe, to avoid getting too close to someone. Sort of like your 'I'm a confirmed bachelor' bullshit."

He chuckled. "We've both been telling ourselves a lot of lies."

"You know I'm still not there, right? I mean, I think I'm pretty screwed up in a lot of ways."

"You think I'm not? We've seen each other at our best and our worst. I'm pretty sure we can handle whatever comes at us."

"Maybe so, but that's not really what I'm talking about. What I mean is, some of those reasons I've given for holding back on this, on us, are actually valid. They aren't lies I've told myself. They're still going to be hurdles."

"You're right. But I've since had my eyes opened to a few facts I'd previously been blind to, and I'm of the belief that there's nothing we can't overcome together."

"What did Pop Pop say to you?"

"Can't you give me some credit for figuring out a few things on my own? Without having to be told?"

She shook her head. "No."

"God, you're annoying." He picked her up. "And funny." He laid her down on her bed. "And beautiful." He came down on top of her, kissing her again as their bodies crushed together. "And sexy as fuck."

"Hunter," she said breathlessly. "I'm being serious."

"I know. And we'll talk about it. Later. Can we at least scale one wall tonight? Because I really want to be inside you."

She sighed. "God. I want that too. So much."

They kissed again. Given how hard his cock was, Hunter was impressed with his ability to be patient, but the truth was he was content to just kiss her. To feel the heat of her breath, to smell and taste the sweet bourbon on her lips. Neither of them reached for more. Not right away.

Ailis turned her face away first, crying uncle. "Please. Take off your clothes."

He grinned as he rose from the bed. Rather than peel off his own clothing, he grasped her hands and pulled her up as well. Tugging her shirt over her head, he bent his, running his lips over her bare shoulder as he unclasped her bra.

Ailis didn't seek to cover herself as he pulled the scrap of lace away, then stepped back to get a better look. He'd never fully appreciated just how big an idiot his former best friend was until this moment, when he saw Ailis without her shirt on.

"Jesus, A."

Her cheeks flushed. She hated the way she blushed, but he loved it. It was actually a turn-on, especially when the color crept down her chest.

"Your turn," she said, reaching to take his shirt off. He beat her there, adding his shirt to hers on the floor. Then he gave her some time to look. She'd seen him bare chested before. Summers were hot. They'd gone swimming together a handful of times, and he'd spent the better part of one muggy afternoon in August changing the sparkplugs in her car, sans shirt.

She stepped closer to run her hands over his shoulders. The touch wasn't enough. He needed skin to skin. He grasped her hips and pulled her toward him until her breasts were pressed against him. Hunter kissed her again.

Neither of them broke apart, even as they started shedding their pants. Hers hit the floor a second before his. Ailis wasted no time exploring with her hands, gripping his bare ass.

His erect cock rubbed against her stomach and things shifted into fast-forward.

"Gotta have you," he murmured against her lips.

"Now," she breathed against his mouth.

They moved together as one unit, connected, as they resumed their places on the bed. Her legs parted. She was ready, but he wasn't going to move them to that level so quickly.

He ran his tongue along her neck and down to her breasts, sucking one of her nipples into his mouth. He recalled how hard she pinched her own nipple on New Year's Eve. The memory prodded him to use his teeth, nipping the tight nub until she gasped.

Her heated response sent his brain straight to kinky land. "You have no idea all the things I want to do to you, Ailis. If you did, I think you'd run."

She smiled. "Or I'd tell you to hurry up and do them. You said I get extra credit for kinky."

"Fuck me," he muttered.

"Hunter," she said.

"Yeah?"

"Hurry up."

He didn't respond to her taunt. Much. Instead, he shifted lower and nipped at her clit.

Her hips jerked, but he anticipated the response, ready for her. He pressed her against the mattress and he continued to drive her insane with his mouth on her pussy.

Her hands found their way to his hair, gripping and pulling until his scalp burned. He wanted more. Hunter drove his tongue inside her and she came apart.

Her head thrashed back and forth as she cried out. He was vaguely aware that he should probably warn her to be a bit quieter, but he wasn't about to stop to issue the advice.

He lifted his head as her orgasm waned. She was breathing heavily, her face flushed. She'd never looked lovelier.

Hunter crawled over her once more and kissed her.

"More," she whispered after several minutes.

He reached over the edge of the bed for his pants, digging a condom out of his wallet. She helped him sheathe himself, then he pressed the head of his cock just inside her.

Ordinarily, once he got to this point, he got down to business. This time, he paused to look at her. He understood just how important this moment was. And as he looked into her blue eyes, he knew she did too.

Unfortunately, he wasn't blind to the fear he saw there too.

"Don't be scared," he whispered.

She started to deny feeling that way. She misunderstood.

He kissed the words away.

Then he clarified. "Of us."

Ailis didn't bother to deny those fears existed. Mr. Collins had been right. Hunter would have to drag her out, prod her along until she figured out the same thing he just had.

They'd both dodged a bullet a year ago.

Hunter kissed her again. And then, because he couldn't resist her a second longer, he pushed inside, one quick, hard thrust that had them both gasping for air, groaning at how good it felt.

He held himself up on his elbows, kissing her yet again.

"You're so beautiful," he murmured.

She smiled, her incredulous expression telling him she believed it was the sex talking. So be it. As far as he was concerned, he had a lifetime to convince her.

He withdrew until just the head of his cock remained inside, then he thrust back in. Ailis wrapped her legs around his waist, tilting her hips so he could slide in even deeper.

He started to move faster, harder, reciting multiplication tables in his head, hoping he could draw this out. Make it last.

She scored his back with her nails, arching against him. She was close too. He reached lower to touch her clit, stroking it, determined to bring her with him.

Within seconds, she was there, her body gyrating beneath his.

"So good," she said, her voice more breath than tone. "So good. God, Hunter."

Damn if Ailis wasn't good for his ego.

"Ailis," he said, his own climax imminent. "Jesus."

Both of them came at almost the exact same time, and their words fell away. Her body clenched, tightening around his dick. He came hard, closing his eyes, feeling his heart beat in unison with each spurt of come filling the condom. The rubbers were going away soon. He didn't want anything between them. Nothing.

She was his.

Ailis Adams was *his*.

Chapter Eight

Hunter looked across the table as Ailis took a sip of wine and wondered what the hell he'd done to deserve so much happiness. It was Valentine's Day, and he'd just advanced to the third round of *February Stars*, coming in third tonight after Rory and Robbie. Of course, his win hadn't been quite as challenging as it might have been if Leah hadn't been a no-show. Regardless of that, he couldn't quite believe he was still in the game.

And that wasn't even the best part about his life at the moment. The best part was nibbling at the crusty bread the waitress had just brought them, grinning at him, still riding the same high he was over tonight's results.

It seemed crazy, but lately his confidence stemmed less from his belief in his own abilities and more from her belief in him. Then he realized his dreams had changed. He still wanted the career in music, but not as a solo act. From this point on, he wanted to be part of a team. An Ailis and Hunter team.

He'd spent the night with her after last week's show, Ailis curled around him like a soft, warm kitten. Unfortunately, by morning, she'd erected the walls and started pulling out all the old excuses again, telling him he needed to concentrate on the competition, insisting that they put the sex stuff on hold until March. She'd held firm to her resolve, rebuffing his advances at every turn.

After the show tonight, he told her in no uncertain terms that they were going out to dinner to celebrate the win and the holiday. What she didn't know yet was that after dinner, she was coming home with him. At this point, he didn't care if he had to kidnap her to get her there.

Her phone pinged and she glanced at the screen, frowning as she read the text.

"Problem?"

"I don't know. Les said he finally got in touch with Leah. She said someone stole her dog, threatened to kill it if she showed up tonight. Apparently, the threat felt serious enough that she stayed away."

"Jesus. Who would do something like that?"

Ailis shrugged. "If Victor was still competing, I would have said him, but…" She paused. Hunter knew where her thoughts had gone, because his had traveled there, too.

"Someone messed with his earpiece."

Ailis leaned back in her chair, concerned. "You're in the show because the top competitor was shoved down a flight of stairs."

Hunter ran a hand through his hair. By now, he would have gotten a haircut, but Ailis was convinced this shaggy look was only adding to his sex appeal. "You don't really think all of this is connected, do you? I mean, the guy falling down the stairs was a mugging. And there's a chance Victor just got a faulty earpiece."

"And Leah?"

He sighed. He didn't have a good reason for what had happened to her. Leah was emotionally fragile; all the competitors were aware of that. But she was talented and she deserved to have her shot. "Threatening her dog was a dirty move on someone's part. Les suspect anyone?"

"His text just says she missed because she was afraid someone would kill the dog. I'm sure he's going to start taking a closer look at everyone who's still involved in the competition. The performers and their managers."

"So we're suspects?"

She shook her head. "No. If it is all connected, the mugging happened before you got involved in the competition."

"Which leaves Rory, Robbie and Wes. And their agents."

Ailis rested her chin on her hand. "I don't think it's Rory, and Robbie doesn't seem the type—too meek. I don't know much about Wes."

"Luckily, it's not our mystery to solve. We have more important things to think about."

Ailis nodded, but seemed less inclined to discuss the current state of their personal relationship. It was obvious Ailis thought time was going to solve her problem before she'd have to make any decisions. In her mind, if—actually, she always said *when*—he won the contest, his career would take off and he would be gone. For some reason, she insisted that was going to be an end, not a beginning. Which he didn't agree with.

Of course, on the other hand, they never discussed what would happen if he lost and life continued as normal. He wondered if she was more afraid of that possibility than his chance at stardom. She had an excuse to push him away if his career took off, pretending she preferred a life that didn't include the wheels on the bus going round and round. If things stayed the same, with him here in Baltimore, where did she see them going then?

He considered asking her, but before he opened his mouth, she launched into what was becoming her standard after-show debriefing. She discussed everything he did right, then listed several things they needed to work on before next week's show. Hunter tried to listen, but he was finding it hard to concentrate. Ailis was wearing a short black skirt and a red V-neck sweater that revealed just enough cleavage to send uncomfortable amounts of blood to his cock.

"So next week, when you— Hunter?"

His gaze flew from her breasts to her face. "Yeah?"

"What did I just say?"

He didn't have a clue, and his silence made that all too apparent.

She rolled her eyes. "Seriously? Did you hear anything I said?"

Hunter shook his head.

Ailis blew out an exasperated breath. "We only have a week to fix this stuff, Hunter. Now is not the time to lose focus."

Ever since his audition, he'd followed Ailis's lead, handed her the reins because when it came to molding his image and his performance, there was no denying she had the knowledge and experience to take him where he needed to go.

However, tonight, he was grabbing the control, showing her that everything wasn't always going to be on her terms.

He leaned forward, reaching across the table to take her hand. "Go to the bathroom, take off your panties, and bring them back to me."

Ailis fell silent for every bit of thirty seconds before she managed to choke out the word, "What?"

"You heard me. We're taking the night off from preparing for the contest."

"But—"

"We're also putting the excuses away. We can pick that fight back up again tomorrow. Tonight, you're earning your extra credit in kinky. You're wearing stockings and garters because you knew I would notice. I did. You want this as much as I do, so let's not pretend or lie to each other."

As was her standard practice, Ailis went quiet as she measured his words and considered her response. When she finally did reply, her answer blew him away. "Okay. No pretending. No lying."

That was all she said before she excused herself to the ladies' room.

Hunter used the time alone at the table mentally preparing a list of everything he wanted to introduce Ailis to. There was very little the two of them hadn't discussed over the past year as their friendship grew, but sex was one subject that she'd remained fairly quiet about. The few comments she'd made painted enough of a picture for him to know that her sexual experiences were extremely limited and very vanilla, but two times in bed with her had proven there was nothing plain about her desires.

When she returned, Ailis walked over to his chair and held her closed hand out. He opened his, accepting the panties she gave him before she returned to her own seat. Hunter slipped them into his pocket, his hand lingering there to touch the silk.

"Your panties give you away. You're wet," he murmured.

"It's been a long week," she replied sardonically.

He chuckled. "Too damn long. And it's your fault. Which means I'm going to have to punish you."

Her cheeks flamed the deepest red he'd ever seen and her eyes were heavy with desire. "Punish?" she whispered.

"When we get back to my place, I'm going to take you over my knee, pull up that skirt and spank you."

She bit her lower lip nervously. "Seriously?"

His smile grew. Tonight was going to be a lot of fun. "Oh yeah. And once those sexy ass cheeks of yours match the color on your face right now, I'm going to fuck you to your first orgasm with my fingers."

"First orgasm?"

Hunter hated the distance between them. He rose and stepped behind her chair. "Stand up for a minute."

She did so, watching as he pulled her chair next to his, then moved her silverware and wine. They were dining late because of the show, so the restaurant wasn't as crowded as it probably had been earlier. They had a table by the window, so he decided to turn her facing the street outside with him, their backs to the room.

Once they reclaimed their seats, he wrapped his arm around the top of her chair, toying with a tendril of her hair that had fallen loose from her sexy up-do.

"Are you on the Pill?"

She nodded. "Yes."

"I've never taken a woman without a condom. Not once. Not even Rhonda. Birth control made her sick."

"I know. College roommates, remember?"

He leaned closer, kissing the shell of his ear before whispering his desire. "I don't want anything between us. I want to come inside you."

She shivered, her eyes drifting closed for just a moment. Then she turned her face to his, giving him a quick kiss. "I want that too."

"Is there anything else you want?"

Ailis leaned closer to him, nestled beneath his arm. "I want to give you a blowjob."

He ran his fingertips along her cheek. "We'll pencil that in after your first orgasm."

She giggled. "I'm getting seriously turned on by your scheduling skills."

"After the blowjob, I'm going down on you. Going to tease that tiny little clit of yours until you're begging me to fuck you."

"I've never had a conversation like this in my life."

He shook his head in amazement. Paul really was a jackass. "Get used to it. And remind me to introduce you to phone sex. You'll love it."

"I love everything you do."

As far as compliments went, Hunter figured that was the best one he'd ever gotten in his life. "Ditto, mouse. You blow me away. Every goddamn day."

She started to shake her head, to dismiss his praise. He cupped her cheek to stop her. "I mean it. You're smart and beautiful. You're the most observant person I've ever met. And the nicest. I can't quite figure out why you hang out with an oaf like me."

She rolled her eyes. "Yeah, right. You're the coolest guy I know. Meanwhile, I'm a big nerd."

"Ailis?"

"Yeah?

"Let me tell you about the third orgasm."

"The third? Did I have the second one already?"

He nodded. "Yep. I'm going down on you, remember?"

She sucked in a deep breath. "How could I forget that?"

"For the third one, we're going to move into my bedroom."

"We weren't in the bedroom yet?"

He chuckled. "There's no way we'll make it to the bedroom until those first couple of orgasms are out of the way. You're lucky I'm not bending you over my knee right here."

Her eyes widened. "You wouldn't dare."

"Maybe not at this table. But I could easily drag you back to the bathroom, lock the door, bend you over the sink and..." He let his words drift away, let her fill in the blanks.

"I've never had sex in public," she admitted.

"But you want to."

She didn't respond. She didn't have to. Her hungry expression told him that was exactly what she wanted.

"Ailis. You have two choices right now. Number one, we act out that restroom fantasy, or two, I pay the bill and we head back to my place to start working on those four orgasms I've promised you."

"Four?" she whispered.

"You're going to have three and four while I'm buried deep inside you in bed. We'll schedule in a fifth tomorrow morning when we wake up."

Her words came halting, her tone breathless. "Check. Home. God, hurry."

Hunter waved for the waitress, saying they'd decided not to order dinner because Ailis wasn't feeling well. Her flushed cheeks helped sell the lie. She really did look feverish. He paid for their drinks and the two of them stood to go.

As they were leaving, Hunter was surprised to spot Paul and Rhonda sitting at a nearby table. He'd been so focused on Ailis, he hadn't seen them. Given Ailis's softly muttered "damn," it was clear she hadn't seen them either.

Hunter was ready to ignore them completely, but Paul had other plans when he stood up and blocked their path.

His former best friend looked pissed as hell, and Hunter wondered if Paul had been watching them as they flirted, kissed and planned their evening. "So you really *are* dating? I'd heard—"

"You heard wrong," Hunter said, tucking Ailis closer. He glanced at the table and saw Rhonda. Her face was pale and she had dark circles under her eyes. Trouble in paradise?

That's when he realized she was drinking a martini. His face must have betrayed his thoughts because she answered his unspoken question.

"I had a miscarriage."

Paul turned toward her, shooting her a dirty look.

"I'm sorry," Ailis said. "So sorry." There was no denying the sincerity in her tone, even after everything Rhonda had done to her.

"Me too," Hunter said, recognizing the anger he'd harbored toward her for the past year was gone. He suspected that had a lot to do with the fact he'd fallen head over heels for Ailis. His life was infinitely better now than it had been with Rhonda. She'd actually done him a favor by running off with Paul.

Rhonda didn't reply. Instead, she took another sip of her martini, ignoring the way her husband was glaring at her.

"We'll leave you to your evening," Hunter said, anxious to get away from the couple. Talk about buzzkill.

Paul didn't move as his gaze traveled from Hunter to Ailis. "Are you still waiting tables at your family's pub?"

"No. Actually, I've moved on to bigger and better things." She looked at him and smiled. "I'm managing the career of a rock star."

Hunter grinned and winked, unable to resist getting his own dig in. "I do like to hear you say I'm bigger and better."

Ailis laughed. "God. You're incorrigible."

Paul clearly didn't like being ignored or insulted. "You're not seriously calling that a career, are you? Tying yourself to a dreamer? Ailis, you need a practical plan. I'm sure Rhonda could put in a word for you at the marketing firm, help you get your job back. After all, it's been a year. I would have hoped you'd moved on."

Hunter stiffened, ready to invite Paul outside for a chat with his fists.

Ailis beat him to the punch. "I haven't just moved on, Paul. I've moved up. You didn't knock me down for long, so don't stand there thinking you're all that and a bag of chips." She looked at Rhonda and gave her a sad smile. "Take care of yourself, Rhonda. I really am sorry. Goodbye, Paul."

She took Hunter's hand and they walked out of the restaurant.

"As much as I enjoyed you telling that son of a bitch off, I still want to go back in there and beat the shit out of him."

"He's not worth it, Hunter. He's too arrogant to get it, with words or fists. I mean, I knew he had an overblown sense of self-worth, but I swear it's gotten worse."

Hunter nodded. "Yeah. You're right. The guy was always cocky, but that," he pointed back toward the restaurant, "that was next-league stuff. Something's off with him."

"And Rhonda. She looked really sad. I know she had a miscarriage so that's completely understandable, but they just looked…"

"Miserable."

She nodded.

Hunter knew what the real issue was with Paul. "I should probably go ahead and point out the obvious. He's jealous as shit that I'm with you."

He thought she would agree, so he was surprised when she shook her head. "No. I'm sure that's not it. I mean, he dumped me. And he was never, not once, jealous when we were dating. He doesn't seem to possess that gene."

She was wrong. Way wrong, but he didn't bother to correct her. As far as he was concerned, they'd already spent too much time thinking about the jackass. Time to get them back on track.

"Ailis."

"Yeah?"

"You ready for your punishment?"

Just like that, the exes were forgotten, and they were right back to where they'd been at the table. They caught a cab, making out like teenagers in the backseat all the way to his place.

Once they were inside his apartment, he closed the door, locked it and twisted her around, pressing her back against it so he could kiss her the way he'd been dreaming about since walking off that stage earlier tonight.

When he'd heard his name and realized he'd made the cut again, all he could think about was her. This moment when he could take her in his arms and prove to her that they were perfect for each other—in and out of the bedroom.

She reached up, intent on wrapping her hands around his neck, but he had other plans. He grasped her wrists and dragged them above her head, holding them with one hand against the door. She shivered in response.

Bondage. He was going to introduce her to it, tie her up. His cock throbbed harder at the thought. Reaching under her soft sweater with his free hand, he cupped her breast, squeezed it through her bra. She tried to twist her head away, seeking a way to breathe. He didn't let her escape. "You're mine, Ailis. Completely."

Ailis lifted one of her legs, wrapping it around his, trying to find a way to pull his cock closer to where she wanted it. "Hunter, please. Take me to your bedroom."

He ran his lips along the side of her neck, then bit her earlobe. "I think you're forgetting something."

When he pulled away, her dazed eyes proved she'd probably forgotten her own damn name, so he reminded her. "Orgasms one and two are happening here. Now."

Before she could reply, he retained his grip on her hands, dragging her farther into his apartment, straight to the couch. He sat down and tugged her into the position he'd described in the restaurant. Self-preservation reared its head as she struggled to escape, even though he knew she wanted what he was offering.

"Ailis. Stop fighting me or this will be a real punishment. Not play." He swatted her ass, just a gentle tap compared to what he planned to give her, and she settled down instantly.

"Real? Play?" She shook her head, her red hair hanging around her face so that he couldn't read her expression. It didn't matter. He knew her well enough to know she was way out of her realm right now.

He drew her skirt up to her waist, revealing the garter he'd spotted the second he'd picked her up tonight for the show. He unclicked the back two snaps. He wanted her ass completely bare for what came next. She shivered, aroused. "Right now, it's play, because you're excited, waiting with bated breath to see what I'll do next."

"Do it," she whispered.

"You're not in charge tonight, A. I'm calling the shots."

Once again, he could almost see the wheels in her brilliant mind struggling to work out what that would mean for her. He decided the best way to handle her tonight was to keep her off-balance. The easiest way to do that was to stop her from thinking.

He spanked her, a hard, sharp slap that was loud in the quiet room.

Ailis tried to rear up, to scramble off his lap. He was ready for her, his left hand pressing firmly on her back, holding her in place.

She grabbed his leg, intent on pushing away. He halted her by placing three more smacks to her ass. He wasn't taking it easy on her. There had been too many clues in their past escapades that told him she liked the bite of pain.

Ailis stopped trying to escape, especially when he ran his fingertips along her slit. God, she was hot as lava and so wet. His cock had been hard since the restaurant and he was tempted to unzip his pants, to give the poor guy some room. Problem with that idea was once it was out, it would go in...*her*.

She'd agreed to no condoms. That fact alone was wreaking havoc on his self-control.

"Jesus," he murmured. He was fighting a losing battle with himself. He'd never wanted a woman this bad.

Ailis looked over her shoulder at him. The woman was too damn smart. For someone with limited sexual experience, she was pretty freaking good at reading his tone and expression. "Rearrange the schedule."

He shook his head, even though rejecting that idea was the last thing on earth he wanted to do. He lifted his hand and spanked her again, harder. Five times, six, seven. Ailis anticipated the blows, raising her ass toward them, inviting him to give her more.

She'd found purchase by gripping his left thigh tightly.

After the tenth smack, he pushed three fingers inside her tight pussy and she cried out loudly, rearing back and forth. She was closer to coming than he realized, than he'd expected.

He thrust his fingers in deeper, until he felt her inner muscles clench. As the first pulse of her orgasm struck, he withdrew his fingers, shoving just one into her ass.

She bucked like an unbroken bronco on his lap, coming hard. And loud. He'd be lucky if his neighbors didn't call the cops. That concern led to a brilliant idea. In addition to the bondage, he was going to gag her.

He slowly stroked that single finger in and out of her ass as her climax began to wane. Once it passed, her grip on his leg relaxed and she hung over him like a limp rag doll.

"One down," he said softly.

She snorted, just one breathy laugh before trying to rise. He helped her, drawing her head to his shoulder once she was upright, cradling her on the lap she'd just been "punished" over.

It was on the tip of his tongue to tell her that he loved her. The words were right there, hovering, clamoring to get out.

But they hadn't spoken them yet. His gut told him she wasn't ready. Not to say them or to hear them. So he choked them back, the taste bitter.

She lay against him for several minutes, her breathing slowing. When she lifted her head, she cupped his cheek and kissed him. One soft, gentle, amazing fucking kiss.

"My turn?"

He was so blown away by how beautiful, how sweetly trusting she looked that he couldn't recall what was on the list next. That oversight was remedied when she slid off his lap, kneeling between his open thighs.

She reached for his zipper, but he beat her there. His cock was too fucking hard, and as much as he wanted her hands on it, delivering the thing safely from anything with sharp teeth was paramount.

Once he'd unzipped his jeans, he stood and moved to her side. "This is a lot easier without denim in the way." He dropped his jeans and boxers, then reclaimed his place on the couch as her gaze remained riveted to his cock.

"Bigger and better," she whispered. He chuckled. That wasn't what she'd meant when she was talking to Paul at the restaurant and it had still felt good to hear.

Now...

He gasped when she wrapped her hand around his cock with a firm grip. There was no hesitance in her movements. She started to stoke him and he realized this wasn't going to take long.

Especially not when she bent her head lower and took the tip into her mouth.

"Fuck. I swear to God, what's about to happen isn't a reflection of my stamina. I want you too bad. You can't make me wait a week again."

She giggled around his cock, sucking him deeper, as if taking his words as a dare to send him over the edge even quicker. He pulled the pins from her hair, setting loose the few strands that hadn't already fallen out. Then he used that silky mass against her, gripping it tightly, using it to pull her closer, then drag her just the smallest distance away.

Ailis let him set the rhythm, relinquishing control. One of her hands retained its grip on the base of his dick, while the other traveled lower, cupping his balls.

"Fucking. Killing. Me," he said through gritted teeth.

She didn't respond. She couldn't. He wasn't giving her any reprieve. Her submission, her willingness to follow his lead, was too much.

"Fuck it," he said, giving up any attempt at prolonging this sweet agony. He tugged her hair harder as he pushed her mouth deeper along his dick. And then he was a goner.

He let go of her, so she could move away if she didn't want him to come in her mouth. He should have known better. Timid Ailis didn't shy away from anything when it came to sex. She tightened her grip on his cock as she drank down every drop of come.

He leaned back against the couch, stroking her hair when she rested her head on his thigh, giving him time to recover.

Once again, he fought the urge to open up, to tell her everything that was written in his heart. He actually opened his mouth to say the words, but she moved, distracting him.

As he watched, she stood and started to disrobe. It wasn't a striptease. It was something so much hotter.

She held his gaze as she drew the soft sweater over her head. Her bra was the same deep red, lacy. It was designed more for seduction and less for support as her breasts were pushed up, creating the kind of cleavage a man dreamed of pushing his dick into. He really wanted to fuck those breasts.

But once again, she diverted his attention when she drew down the zipper of her skirt and shimmied it off.

She was still wearing her stockings, the front two clips firmly in place even as the back two dangled loose. Ailis slipped off her shoes, unhooked the garter and dragged it and the stockings off.

Her bra was the last to go.

Neither of them had spoken a word as she'd undressed. Once she was completely naked, she stood in front of him, her hands hanging at her sides, his view unhindered.

How much courage must it take for her to stand there, naked, silent, in front him?

He stood, needing to touch as he looked. His gaze traveled the length of her and back up again as he reached out to grip her hips, to hold her there. His.

"You're the most beautiful woman I've ever seen."

As he expected, she gave him that damned disbelieving smile and tiny shake of her head.

He'd let that response slide one time too many.

Hunter gripped her chin, forcing her face up to look at him. "You're the most beautiful woman I've ever seen," he repeated.

This time, her eyes narrowed in confusion.

"Hunter," she whispered uncertainly.

He leaned down and placed his lips against her ear. "You're the most beautiful woman I've *ever* seen. You're mine, Ailis. I'm never going to let you go."

She stiffened slightly at his admission. So much for shielding his feelings. It simply wasn't possible with her.

And even if it did freak her out, he didn't care. He wasn't giving up on them, regardless of her excuses, her fears. They'd overcome them all and maybe then she'd understand exactly what she meant to him. Paul had abused her trust, but more than that, he'd shaken her self-confidence. Ailis was an intelligent woman who'd let her heart do the thinking in that first relationship, despite her better judgment. It was going to be difficult to convince her to do that again, to get her to take that leap of faith, trusting that he wouldn't hurt her, wouldn't leave her.

"Hunter. Please. Take me to bed."

He'd promised her one more orgasm in the living room, but schedules be damned. Maybe she was hesitant to lose herself in him, but he didn't suffer the same fear. He wanted to drown in her.

He clasped hands with her and led her to his room. The optimist in him was determined they'd be here tonight, so he'd tidied his entire apartment and put clean sheets on the bed prior to heading to the show. Not that he expected Ailis to notice that at the moment.

However, there was one thing he knew she'd see.

She gasped when they stepped into his bedroom and he lit the candle he'd put out on his nightstand. For the first time in his life, Hunter had been bitten by the same romantic bug he usually gave other guys shit about. He'd scattered red rose petals all over the duvet.

He put his phone next to the candle and fired up the music he'd selected. The first song, "All I Can See", was a new one he'd written a few weeks ago before his talk with Mr. Collins. Before he'd managed to see what had been staring him right in the face for months.

He recorded it this morning on some cheap equipment he had in his place. The quality wasn't the best, but it was good enough.

Ailis hadn't heard this song yet because he hadn't known how to sing it to her without giving away he'd written it for her.

She sank down on the edge of the mattress as she listened, her eyes closed. He stood there, his gaze locked on her face. He didn't sit next to her because part of him wanted to be ready to block the door if she tried to bolt.

There was no way to deny he'd written it for her when he sang about the lion within the mouse. It was a song about love and loss, then finding something you'd never noticed, something you never knew was there, and discovering a better person at the other end.

It wasn't until the song ended that he realized he'd been holding his breath.

When she opened her eyes and looked at him, there were tears on her lashes.

"That's..." She paused, as if struggling to speak. "My God, Hunter. I don't know what to say."

"You like it?"

"It's amazing. I've never...heard..." She wiped away a tear as it slid down her cheek.

He sat next to her on the edge of the bed and took her hand. It was odd when he realized they were both naked. It felt natural to be here with her like this. The moment had grown too heavy, too steeped in things they weren't quite ready for.

"Lay on your back, A. We're behind schedule."

She grinned, but managed to get the last word. "Thank you. For the song." She kissed him quickly. Then she scooted to the middle of the bed and lay down.

He crawled over her, adding his own kiss to the mix before making the journey south. He took his time, enjoying the sights along the way. The mountains of her breasts, the valley between. She laughed when he added his travelogue narrative in with his kisses, sucks and licks.

When he finally reached his destination, he lifted his head and winked at her. "Time to check into the hotel." With that, he pressed his tongue inside her. Her quiet laughter quickly turned to soft sighs that encouraged him to keep going.

He fucked her with his tongue as he stroked her clit. Then he switched, pressing two fingers inside as he sucked the tiny nub into this mouth.

Her hands tangled in his hair, and twice she giggled when his scruffy five o'clock shadow tickled her. She was just on the verge of coming when he pulled away.

She narrowed her eyes. "You promised me my second orgasm would come that way."

"I also said it would happen in the living room. Never been good with a schedule."

She rolled her eyes at the inanity of his comment. He was notorious for being late and they both knew it. "I know."

"But I'm very good at spontaneous." As he spoke, he moved back up her body until they were nose to nose, her breasts pressed against his chest, his hard cock nestled between her outstretched thighs.

They kissed once more, then he pulled away to look at her. "You sure you're okay if—"

"Come inside me," she murmured.

He placed the head of his cock at her opening and then he slid his way into heaven. Once he was completely in, he paused, sucking in a much-needed breath. "I know we've done this before, but..."

"It feels different this way. Closer. Better."

He nodded, unable to express all the other feelings crashing in on him. There were too many—all jumbled together. Feelings of love, possession, desire. Longing for forever, marriage, babies.

Ailis must have recognized his turmoil. She managed to make it all go away with a mischievous grin and a joke. "You keep promising me kinky, but all I get is romance. Not that I'm complaining, it's just—"

He kissed her before she could finish. "In other words, get on with it, right?"

"Just pick one and roll with it, hotshot. I'm not getting any younger here."

He laughed, even as he withdrew and thrust back in. Then because she'd basically dared him, he lifted her hands and pressed them to the mattress by her head, taking her harder. Deeper. Faster.

She was right on the verge of coming when he pulled out.

Her temper erupted. "What the—!"

He twisted her to her stomach, dragging her up on her knees and pushing back in from behind.

She obviously approved of the new position as she placed her hands on the headboard, using her arms to add even more force to their almost brutal thrusting. Romance be damned. He was fucking her like a man possessed, his fingers digging deeply into her hips as he used his grip to drive her against him harder.

For the third time, he left her dangling on the edge with a hasty retreat.

"I swear to God—" she started, just before he turned her once more. He knelt with his legs spread out, dragging her to face him.

"Open your legs and sink down on me. Wrap your legs around my waist. I want to see your face when you come."

She shifted into place, sliding back onto his cock slower, ready to add her own brand of torment to the game. Once he was seated to the hilt, he cupped her ass cheeks and held her still.

They were face-to-face, pelvis to pelvis, breasts to chest, connected everywhere. It wasn't physically possible for them to get any closer and still remain two separate bodies. Even so, he wanted more.

"Tell me you're mine," he demanded.

"Hunter."

"I know what you think, what you believe. And maybe you aren't ready for this, even though I know you are. So for tonight, I'll let you pretend. Say it even if you think it's a lie. I want you to practice, want you to hear it, so you'll start to see I'm right."

"Please don't—"

"Say you're mine, Ailis. Say it now."

"You're mine."

He grinned. It wasn't what he meant and she knew it, but that didn't stop it from sounding pretty damn good. "You're right. I am."

"And I'm yours."

The last slipped out in a whisper, and he suddenly regretted not knowing if she was finally giving in and admitting the truth, or just pretending as he'd requested.

"Always," he added. It didn't matter if she meant it or not. The feelings were there regardless.

He lifted her then, drawing her upwards until just the tip of his cock remained inside, then he released her, and she dropped back down heavily. Both of them groaning at the impact. He repeated the motion over and over until they were panting, scratching, clawing. He pushed her to her back on the bed one last time and pounded inside her, desperate to make sure she felt this fucking for a long time. Forever.

He wanted her to feel him imprinted inside her for the rest of her life. Their life.

She drew blood as she scratched his back, holding back nothing, demanding more.

"Harder!" she yelled. "God, Hunter. Please!"

He'd never taken a woman with so much force, but she wouldn't let him slow down or hold back. She wanted it all, and that was what she was going to get.

She came a split second before him, her inner muscles constricting on his cock, leaving him no choice but to follow her down.

Neither of them moved for several minutes after. Now that common sense and sanity was returning, he was terrified he'd hurt her.

"Ailis," he murmured, forcing himself to look at her.

"I want to do that again." Her gaze was steady, focused, crystal clear.

He smiled. "Can you give me a year or two to recover from that one?"

She shook her head. "An hour. Tops. Maybe thirty minutes. And I want more kinky stuff next time."

Hunter laughed, glancing around his room. "I'm on it. Pretty sure I own enough ties and belts to bind you to this bed spread-eagle," he promised, though even as he spoke, he knew with her, it was always going to be more romance than kink.

She sucked in an excited breath. "Changed my mind. Fifteen minutes. Not a second more."

He rolled to her side, pulling her until she was nestled in his arms, her eyes closed, and she started breathing deeply, a sign of total relaxation—or maybe exhaustion.

"Fifteen minutes, mouse," he murmured, even though he knew they'd be asleep long before that.

As he lay there, he played the song he'd written for her over in his head, letting "All I Can See" lure him into the deepest sleep of his life.

Chapter Nine

Ailis stepped out onto the sidewalk and sucked in a deep breath of the cool, fresh air. It felt like winter had decided to retreat early. For one brief day, she could almost pretend this burst of warmth and sunshine signaled spring.

Tonight was the third night of the competition and she was on the wrong side of town, thanks to Robbie spilling coffee on Hunter's outfit for tonight. It had obviously been an accident, but Robbie had winced and jerked away like Hunter was going to punch him for it or something. They'd assured him it was fine, then she told Hunter to stay put at the Soundstage in his stained shirt, and she'd hightailed it back to his place to pick up the outfit they'd earmarked for the last night's competition if needed. Mercifully, the mishap had occurred with hours to spare. They'd driven to the concert venue shortly after lunch, intending to spend the entire day there prepping.

If—no, when—Hunter made it through tonight's competition, they would have to buy something else to wear for the finale.

She'd spent every night at Hunter's since Valentine's Day, and the things they'd done—in his bedroom, kitchen, living room, shower and once in the hallway—had heat creeping to her cheeks, even though she was alone.

Every night, he demanded that she tell him she was his, always with that promise that she could just pretend if it wasn't true. She always gave him the words. And it wasn't a pretense. She'd fallen completely in love with him—and it terrified her.

For six years, she'd wrapped her life around Paul's, living where he wanted to live, hanging out with his friends, working at a job that fit their relationship. She'd molded herself to fit what he needed.

Wouldn't the same hold true for Hunter? For God's sake, she'd spent the better part of the last two months working her ass off to make his dreams come true. *His* dreams.

And if he achieved his goal, found fame and fortune, where did that leave her?

She knew where. Following around behind him.

For some reason, that didn't scare her as much as it had a few weeks earlier. Hunter wasn't Paul, but she was struggling to figure out what the difference was.

Taking a deep breath, she shook off all the worries. She didn't have time to stress out about this right now.

"Ailis."

She turned around at the sound of the familiar voice, hoping she'd misheard. She hadn't. Paul was there, without Rhonda.

"Hi," she said, wondering what it was she'd ever seen in the man. His hair was thinning and already graying at the temples. He looked as humorless as ever. When she thought back, she realized she'd often shared that same serious expression. Nowadays, it felt as if she couldn't wipe the smile off her face.

"I thought that was you. Stopped by the pub, but your cousin Padraig said you'd been staying here lately."

Padraig was obviously trying to make it clear to Paul that she was off-limits. "Why were you at the pub?"

"I wanted to see you."

"Me?" she asked. "Why?"

"Would you join me for a cup of coffee?"

The last thing she wanted to do at this moment was go anywhere with Paul. She'd avoided talking to the man alone for the past year. She saw no reason to break the streak now.

"I'm on my way to the show."

"*February Stars?*"

She nodded.

"Hunter's still in the competition?" he asked.

"Yes. I wasn't under the impression you knew about that."

"Kind of hard to miss these days. It's all over the local news, even saw a piece about it on a national network last night."

"So you know I'm busy. I really need to get going." And then, because she thought it would help move things along, she added, "Shouldn't you be home with your wife? You know, the one you couldn't wait to leave me for?" The old Ailis, the eternal peacemaker who avoided conflict like the plague, would never had been so bitchy, which was apparent by Paul's frown. Knowing him, he'd probably assumed she'd happily trail along after him to wherever he'd wanted to go.

His expression softened. "I only need twenty minutes. Please."

"What is this about?"

"The Daily Grind is just at the end of the block. We can pop in there and grab a table."

She glanced at her cell phone. There was still ninety minutes before the show, and Hunter was the last performer on the schedule. Even so, this wasn't somewhere she wanted to be. "Five minutes. It's all I can spare." She wasn't sure she could stomach any more of him than that.

He smiled like the cat who ate the canary and she instantly regretting giving in. They walked the length of the block in silence.

When they entered, he asked if she wanted something. She shook her head. "I don't have time."

He didn't take that as a hint, so she wound up waiting at a table while he ordered a black coffee with two sugars. Same thing. Every time. Meanwhile, Hunter had made it a game to work his way down the extensive menu, trying every single hot beverage. The last time they'd come in, he'd ordered a CaraMochaNut espresso.

Paul returned to the table. He'd managed to squander the first four minutes of his time without saying a word to her.

"Okay. Let's have it."

"I'm concerned about your relationship with Hunter."

She had two options—dump the hot coffee he'd just bought in his lap or laugh. She chose to laugh, simply because it was less messy. "And on that note, I'll be going."

She started to stand, but he gripped her wrist, holding her in her seat. She tugged it away from his grasp angrily.

"Wait, Ailis. Please. Dammit. I'm messing this up. I meant to start with I'm sorry."

She considered all the apologies he owed her and tried to figure out what his blanket sorry was meant to cover. "You'll have to be more specific."

He winced. "You're right. I do. Truth is, I'm sorry for all of it, but that one was meant for the way I behaved last week at the restaurant."

"Okay." That was probably the easiest thing to forgive him for. Hell, it was actually the *only* thing she'd forgive him for.

"Hunter's doing well in this competition."

She nodded. "Yeah. He is."

"You think he really has a shot at making it as a musician?"

"I do."

"Where does that leave you?"

She scowled. Her future plans were none of his damn business. "I'm not having this conversation with you, Paul."

"Don't you think you'd be smarter to stay in Baltimore, closer to your family? You hated life on the road."

She hadn't, but she had said that to him when he'd expressed a desire to put down roots in Baltimore.

"I meant what I said about your chances of getting back on at the marketing firm. Rhonda says your name comes up all the time. Everyone misses you."

"I'm not going back there."

He sighed. "I was hoping enough time had passed that you would be able to…"

"To what? Work with Rhonda again? No," she said hotly. "Moving on or not, there's no amount of time passing that will make that happen."

"I miss you." His confession came out of left field and pissed her off.

She scoffed. "Oh, sweet Jesus. I really don't have time for this."

"Rhonda's not like you. We don't have much in common. I miss our talks, the way we could discuss the news and politics and medicine. All Rhonda cares about is fashion and makeup. She watches reality TV, for God's sake."

"What did you expect, Paul? It's not like you didn't know her before you took off to Vegas."

"She looked up to me, thought I was smart, special. It felt like she needed me."

"What's that supposed to mean?"

"It's nice to be needed, Ailis. Looked up to, respected. You've always been so self-assured, capable of handling yourself," he swallowed heavily before adding, "smarter than me."

She grinned. "How did that taste?"

He ignored her jest and she wondered briefly if he even got it. That was one of the greatest things about Hunter. The way they could tease each other, make each other laugh.

"You made me better. I didn't realize it at the time, but I can see it now."

Which drove home the truth. She hadn't imagined it. She had given up her own identity to support Paul's. And while she was supporting Hunter's career as well, fighting tooth and nail to help him succeed, it wasn't the same thing. "None of this really matters anymore."

Paul sighed. "If he wins, I think you should just let him go."

"He *is* going to win."

"Then let him go. I hurt you, Ailis. I'll regret that until the day I die. I don't want to see you suffer that same pain again. Hunter's a bad bet."

"He was your best friend."

"You're right. He was. Which means I know him. I don't want you to upend your life for him only to find yourself where I am right now. Stuck in a relationship with a mismatch. You and Hunter have even less in common than Rhonda and I do. You'll both be bored and I hate to see you settle."

"Settle?" That word was completely wrong when it came to her relationship with Hunter, but Ailis recalled feeling as if she'd been settling with Paul. Yep. Two totally different things.

Man, she hadn't wanted to talk to Paul, but she was suddenly glad she had. The whole damn thing had been enlightening, illuminating things that should have been obvious to her if she hadn't been so bunkered down in self-preservation mode. She owed Hunter a big-ass apology.

"Yes. Settle. You were both hurt by me and Rhonda, so you found each other. It was easy and convenient, but that doesn't make it right."

"You're wrong."

He scowled. Paul had never liked being told he was wrong about anything and, even though he was obviously trying to be on his best behavior, his true nature slipped out. "No. I'm not. He wants to be a rock star and he sees you as his easy ticket to the top."

She leaned closer, not wanting to raise her voice, even though a large part of her wanted to rail at him at the top of her lungs. "He's not using me. But *you* did. And those days are over."

She rose and turned to leave, but before she'd taken a step, Paul spoke again. "I'm leaving her."

"What?"

"Maybe…if the baby had lived, we could have found a way to make it work. I was willing to try for our child. Now, it feels like we're fighting for nothing. I never should have left you."

She held her hand up. "Let me stop you there. You did me a favor when you left with Rhonda. I'm sorry your marriage is falling apart, but I don't have a horse in that race anymore and I couldn't care less."

"What's happened to you? The Ailis I fell in love with was compassionate, caring. This is Hunter's influence, isn't it? Suddenly you're sarcastic and—"

"Happy." The word slipped out easily. She was happy. For the first time in her adult life. "I'm happy, Paul."

"You're making a mistake," he called out after her, but she didn't stop, didn't care if he got the last word.

Ailis stepped out of the coffee shop, annoyed and later than she wanted to be. Her car was parked two blocks away, so she started walking faster. The Soundstage was only a ten-minute drive and she had plenty of time, but right now, it felt like the coffee shop was light-years away. All she wanted was to be with Hunter, to let him wrap her up in that big warm embrace of his and soak up his scent.

Perhaps if she'd been a bit calmer, she would have been paying better attention as she waited to cross the street. She would have noticed the car that jumped the curb and clipped her from behind.

When she opened her eyes, two things were instantly apparent. One, her whole body hurt, and two, Paul was kneeling next to her, holding her hand.

"The ambulance is on the way, Ailis. I've done a quick check and I don't think anything is broken, but you're going to have a hell of a bruise on your hip and I'm pretty sure you have a concussion."

"What…happened?"

"Car took the turn too sharp, I guess. Came out of nowhere. Driver didn't stop and no one got the license plate. The owner of the coffee shop is in there right now, checking out the video feed of his outside camera to see if he can find anything for the cops. I swear to God, when I saw that car, saw you rolling over the hood of it, the way you hit your head on the sidewalk, I think I just lost twenty years off my life."

"Call Hunter."

Paul paused, and she thought for a second he was going to refuse her request. "I will if you want me to, but, Ailis, it's almost showtime."

Shit. There was no way Hunter would stick around to compete if he knew she'd been hit by a car. She recalled Leah and the threat to her dog. Obviously, someone was playing to win in this competition. They wanted it badly enough that they didn't care who they hurt.

"Don't call him."

Paul looked far too pleased by her change of heart. Smug bastard thought he was getting his way somehow. Of course, he couldn't see that her request was because she didn't want Hunter to lose his shot at winning, especially considering the fact that, while she was sore from head to toe, she wasn't in any mortal danger.

"Where's my phone?"

Paul looked around for her purse, then accepted it from one of the countless bystanders who'd formed a circle around her, curious to witness whatever came next. "Here. I picked it up," the woman said. "It flew nearly ten feet."

Paul dug around for her phone, but didn't hand it to her. Probably because she was still lying on the ground and fighting like the devil not to vomit. Black spots were dancing in her eyes, and she wasn't sure she could see the screen well enough to make her call. "Can you look for Les's number? Dial it for me?"

Paul nodded and she realized he still knew the code for her iPhone. She should probably change that. He found Les in her contacts. "You want to call him? I can type out a text if you want."

She started to shake her head, then groaned at the piercing pain the movement provoked. "Just dial it and give it to me." She dug deep for the strength to keep her voice steady. If she didn't play this right, Hunter wouldn't be the only man deserting the show and flying to the hospital.

A siren sounded in the distance. She was running out of time.

"Where the hell are you?" Les asked when he answered.

"Fender bender."

"Are you okay?"

"Is that Ailis?" she heard Hunter ask in the background. "What happened?"

"Tell him nothing is wrong. I was in too big a hurry to get back and tapped the bumper of the guy in front of me," she lied. "He's insisting we wait for the police and we still need to exchange insurance information. Tell Hunter I might not make it there in time to see him go on."

Les didn't sound completely convinced when he said, "Okay, I will."

"Good." The ambulance was there, the siren screeching. "There are the cops. Gotta go," she said, disconnecting the phone before Les could question her any further.

Paul gave her a look she couldn't define, a pretty good mix of horrified and surprised. "Wow. Cool liar, Ailis. Didn't know you had that in you."

Of course, he didn't. Paul thought she was too boring, too predictable, too much of a good girl to ever be untruthful.

But she didn't have a chance to call him out for it or to tell him to go away. She was surrounded by three EMTs, while two cops had arrived and were trying to get the crowd to disperse.

Paul was quick to point out he was a doctor and tell them about his own quick assessment of her injuries, which she had to admit were probably correct. Her hip seemed to have absorbed the real blow. The rest of her aches and pains were less severe and due to her brief journey across the hood of a car and her none-too-gentle splash to the pavement.

She didn't remember hitting her head, but she must have, to have blacked out the way she had. It would also explain the pain and sensitivity to any light.

The EMTs secured her to a backboard, then strapped her to the gurney. She was about to ask for her purse when Paul climbed into the ambulance.

"You don't have to come with me."

"Don't be silly," he said, dismissing her words as if they were nothing. She was about to insist, but he pulled her phone back out of her purse. "You got a text while the EMTs were checking you out."

"From who?"

"Les. He said he knows you were lying and that you better have a damn good reason for it."

"Shit." Then she glanced at the EMT. "How long do you think this whole trip is going to take? Is it really necessary?"

The more time passed, the better she started to feel. If she ignored the blinding headache and excruciating pain in her hip.

"Seriously? You just got hit by a car, lady. Once you go through x-rays and see the doctor, the cops are going to want to question you. You've got hours to go, so why don't you try and relax?"

"I don't suppose I could convince you guys to make a stop by the Baltimore Soundstage. It would only take an hour or two."

The man chuckled. "You got tickets to *February Stars*? Man, rough break. Who you rooting for? I think Rory Summit is going to take the whole thing."

She closed her eyes, grateful for the man's attempts at distracting her. "You're crazy. Hunter Maxwell will be the last man standing."

Once they arrived at the hospital, Ailis's patience was stretched thin. Probably because nothing had gone quickly. She wasn't sure how much time had passed, but she was becoming testier and more impatient by the minute.

Everything had played out exactly like the EMT had told her. She'd endured the x-rays and the exam with Paul hovering nearby, conferring with the doctor, as if he was her personal physician or something. It didn't help that Paul was friends with the doctor, and he recalled that he and Ailis had dated.

The cops had just left after a brief interview. It wasn't like she had anything to say. She hadn't seen the car coming, nor could she describe the driver or the vehicle. And while she had this nagging suspicion her accident wasn't really an accident, she didn't admit that to the cops because she didn't want them leaving her and heading over to the Soundstage to start questioning people there—Hunter included—about her injuries in the hit-and-run they didn't know about.

She glanced at the clock hanging in the room. Dammit. It was later than she'd realized. The competition would be over by now, the finalists revealed. She prayed to God Hunter had made it to the next round.

"Where's my phone?" she asked once the cops were gone.

Paul hesitated to give it to her. She'd told him no less than half a dozen times he could leave, but the bastard wouldn't budge.

Now that everything was over and done with, she really needed to let Hunter know she was okay.

"Give me my phone."

He sighed but handed it over.

There were twenty-seven text messages, twelve missed calls, and eight voicemails in total. Four texts were from Les asking where she was and two from Padraig—who was working the pub and completely in the dark about her whereabouts—asking her who had won because the wi-fi had gone down just minutes before the big announcement.

The other twenty-one texts—as well as all the calls and voicemails—were from Hunter, and she could map his entire emotional journey through them. He'd started out worried about her tardiness to the show and then about the fender bender. That had turned to elation when he'd apparently performed the best set of his career. Then she got the nervous, waiting-for-the-results, where-the-hell-are-you strand of messages. The best one had been the "I'm in the finale!" text.

But that happiness had been brief, giving way to pure fear as his last seven messages and two voicemails were pleas for her to contact him and let him know she was okay.

She immediately dialed his number.

"Ailis!" he shouted into the phone. "Thank God. Where the hell are you? I'm at the pub and no one even knew you weren't at the show."

"Hunter, I don't want you to get upset." Even as she said it, she knew he was going to lose his shit when she told him what had happened and that she'd lied.

His voice went dangerously low. "Where the fuck are you?"

"Mercy Medical."

"The hospital? Are you fucking kidding me?!" He yelled so loud she pulled the phone away from her ear.

Paul chuckled, something that only made things worse.

"Who's there with you?" Hunter asked.

There was no way she was having that conversation with him on the phone. "Can you just come get me? I think I talked them out of making me spend the night."

"Talked them out of it? Jesus. I'm on my way. Don't move."

She laughed even though he'd already hung up. Yeah. If she'd had any control over her whereabouts tonight, she would have limped into the Soundstage hours ago.

"He's on his way. You can leave now."

"I don't mind staying until—"

"I swear to God, Paul, if you don't get the fuck out, I'm going to call those cops back and tell them you were the one driving the car just so they'll arrest you and get you the hell away from me."

"You know, I'm just here because I was worried about you."

She sighed. As much as the man annoyed her, she could tell he was being sincere. "I know. I appreciate everything you did for me today. I really do. But I'm fine now. Hunter is on his way."

"You really care about him, don't you?"

She nodded.

"I hope you know what you're doing."

"I do."

He left without saying goodbye, but she wasn't alone for long. Hunter must have broken every speed limit set forth by the city of Baltimore to get there as quickly as he had.

"Ailis." He rushed toward the bed. She was sitting up, grateful for the painkillers the doctor had prescribed. The throbbing in her hip was now just a dull thud, and while her head still ached, it wasn't the blinding, piercing pain she'd suffered from earlier.

"You're in the finale," she said, reaching out to hug him.

He stopped a few feet short of her outstretched arms. "You lied."

"I didn't want you to miss the show."

"You were hit by a fucking car, Ailis."

She winced. "Who told you?"

"Paul was waiting for me outside."

Her temper snapped. "Oh my God, he's an asshole! I told him to leave."

Hunter's voice went instantly calm, something that worried her more than his initial anger. "If he was an asshole, he would have left you on that sidewalk. I'm glad he stayed with you. At least you weren't alone."

"I know you're upset with me, but if you'll just listen to my reasons for—"

"No. I already know your reasons. You don't need to run through them for me. What I need you to do is listen to what I have to say."

She bit her lower lip nervously. "Hunter—" she started.

"Goddammit, Ailis. Be quiet."

She giggled. "No one's ever told me to do that before." She hadn't really meant to make the joke, but she was tired and achy and she just wanted him to take her home, crawl into bed with her and hold her until she fell asleep.

Hunter grinned, even though she knew he was still upset. He sobered up quickly. "No show, no contest, nothing. *Nothing* is more important to me than you. Do you understand that?"

It had been a long, painful, horrible day, and despite it all, she'd never shed a tear.

Until then.

She started to swipe her eyes, not wanting to let them fall, but Hunter was there first, his hands cupping her cheeks tenderly as he bent down to give her a soft kiss.

"I'm sorry," she whispered. "So sorry."

"It's okay, mouse. It's my fault for not making that clear before now. For letting you pretend this is less than it is. I know you're scared, but we gotta find a way to move you beyond that, because I hate that you've been here without me all damn night."

"You'd already made it clear."

"What?"

"None of this is your fault. I don't want you to say that. I don't even want you to think that. I know how you feel about me."

He tugged her into his arms, keeping the embrace loose, gentle, unwilling to hurt her. "I'm so damn glad you're okay. When I think about how much worse this could have been, I go nuts."

"I'm alright. Honest. Bumps and bruises. Doctor said I can go home."

He pulled away and studied her face as if trying to decide if she was lying.

She cataloged her injuries in hopes of setting his mind at ease. "My head hurts and you're really not going to like the look of the bruise on my hip, but nothing's broken or bleeding, I promise."

Hunter sighed. "Okay."

Time for some distraction. "Who's in the finale with you?"

"Rory."

Ailis wasn't surprised, but that outcome didn't really solve the mystery of who was endangering the other contestants in hopes of winning. "I still don't think it's her behind all of this."

Hunter shrugged, unconvinced. "She's the only one who knows for sure that our relationship goes beyond the realm of musician and agent. She'd know that if anything happened to you, I'd rush to your side, show or not."

"Maybe so, but her winning a place in the finale doesn't automatically make her the guilty party. We didn't behave as expected. You didn't get called away to come to the hospital. You still went onstage. So that means Wes and Robbie are suspects in my mind too."

"Yeah. By the way, that reminds me," Hunter reached for her phone on the bedside table, "call Les. He's freaking out."

"Which means my parents are freaking out."

"And your family. I'd just walked into Pat's Pub with Les, looking for you, when you called me. You've got some 'splaining to do, Lucy," he said in a dead-on impersonation of Ricky Ricardo.

She would have laughed if she wasn't feeling so guilty about making her family worry. She scrolled through her lists of contacts and called Tris. If everyone was at the bar, he'd be the best one to spread the news. He had this big, booming voice that meant he could answer everyone's questions in one fell swoop without instigating a game of telephone, where the facts became more fiction with each retelling.

"I'll see about getting you sprung from the joint while you take care of that. Make sure they know you're going home with me tonight. I'm not taking you back to the dorm."

"Okay."

After she explained what happened to Tris, and answered the four hundred and seventy-two questions shouted out by her cousins, aunts, uncles and Pop Pop, she called her parents to assure them she was fine and that Hunter would be taking care of her tonight.

Then she called Les and apologized. Of everyone she'd spoken to since the accident, he was the only one who seemed to understand why she'd lied. She wasn't sure, but she thought the man sounded downright proud of her actions, which drove home two things—what she'd done was wrong and she was born to be a manager.

"Everything's taken care of on my end," Hunter said as he walked back into her room. "How about yours?"

She nodded, then looked at his coffee-stained T-shirt. "Please tell me you weren't wearing that onstage."

He chuckled. "Nope. Paid a guy in the crowd twenty bucks to let me borrow his shirt for the show. We switched back after."

Hunter helped her change from the hospital gown they'd forced her to put on and back into her street clothes. He winced when he saw her hip, and again when he spotted the dirt on her clothing from her rough tumble to the curb.

He wrapped his arm around her shoulders as they walked to the car.

"Find it hard to believe Paul's presence at the accident was a coincidence," he said after they'd gotten in and he'd started driving them home.

"Ran into him out on the street. He'd been coming to your place to talk to me."

Hunter frowned. "About what?"

Now that the adrenaline from the accident and the stress of facing Hunter had drained out, Ailis struggled to keep her eyes open. It had been a long day.

"He apologized for last week, warned me you and I were a bad match, said he regretted breaking up with me, and told me he's leaving Rhonda."

"Jesus. Try not to drop all the bombs at once, A."

She grinned. "No bombs there. None of it matters to me. I'm exactly where I want to be right now."

He wiggled his eyebrows. "Is that right?"

"Bigger and better, remember?"

Hunter reached over and took her hand, giving it a friendly squeeze. "Not tonight. Tonight's going to be slower and softer. All you're getting is a hot bath and some gentle cuddling."

"I really like the sound of that," she said sleepily.

"Close your eyes and rest, mouse. We'll be home soon."

While his apartment wasn't really her home, the word still felt right. Simply because Hunter would be there.

Home.

Chapter Ten

Ailis laughed as she and Hunter entered the bar and the place erupted in applause. Pop Pop had decided to host a party for the two remaining finalists the night before the competition.

Rory had clearly arrived earlier and was surrounded by more than a fair number of supporters. Despite Hunter's concerns that Rory could be the one instigating the "accidents and threats," Ailis refused to believe the woman was guilty.

That feeling grew when Rory spotted them and smiled. She peeled herself away from the crowd to come over and greet them.

"Hard to believe we were joking about the finale just a few weeks ago and now here we are," she said, lifting her beer to Hunter in an unspoken toast.

He nodded. "As I recall, you were mixed up about the outcome."

Rory rolled her eyes good-naturedly. "Guess we'll see who was mixed up tomorrow night. I just wanted to take a minute before everything goes crazy with the finale to say it's been a pleasure competing against you. You're an amazing musician, Hunter, and I seriously hope we have a chance to perform together sometime."

Hunter reached out to shake her hand. "I'd love to play with you, Rory. Been a huge fan of yours for years. Still have quite a few Road Rebels songs in my playlist."

Ailis noticed Rory's smile faded a bit when Hunter mentioned her former band. She'd mentioned they'd split up after a breakup between her and the guitarist, Eddie. Ailis couldn't help but wonder if Rory was nursing a broken heart or if she missed her band. Going solo wasn't an easy thing. Ailis could remember her dad telling her how hard it had been to split from The Universe. She believed that was true now, as she saw his over-the-top excitement about the reunion tour.

"Hey, Hunter!" Tris called out from the bar. "Come grab this Guinness I poured for you before it gets warm."

Hunter walked away, leaving Ailis alone with Rory.

"You doing okay?" Rory asked. "I was worried when I heard about the hit-and-run."

"I'm fine. My skin sort of looks like some tie-dye experiment gone horribly wrong, given all the different shades of bruising, but the soreness is gone."

"I'm glad. I was just talking to Les about it today. I still can't figure out if the man was warning me to be careful or telling me he was on to me."

Ailis laughed. "That sounds like Les."

"So he really doesn't have a clue who's behind any of it?"

"No," Ailis sighed. "My uncle Aaron is a Baltimore cop, and he's been investigating, but no leads so far. Everything has been so random. I think it's hard to conclusively tie any of it together."

"At least Leah got her dog back," Rory said.

"Seriously? I didn't know that. When?"

Rory grinned. "The asshole who stole him tied him to a bike rack outside some dive motel on the edge of the city. The night manager heard him barking and called the number on the dog tag."

"Let me guess, the motel had no cameras."

"You got it."

"Do you think whoever it is gave up and that's why they dumped the dog? The finale is between you and Hunter and neither one of you is behind this, so it's game over, right? The bad guy lost."

Rory tilted her head. "Why are you so sure it's not me? I mean, it's not, and I'm wicked glad you believe me, but still...I'm one of the few no one has tried to sabotage."

Ailis shrugged. "I just know it's not you. You don't think Hunter is involved, right?"

Rory shook her head vehemently. "Hell no, Hunter's a good guy. There's no way he'd stoop to cheating. Besides, there's no way I'd suspect him after that hit-and-run. The guy worships the ground you walk on. He's not about to put you in harm's way."

Ailis felt her cheeks flush. "I'd hardly say he worships the ground I walk on."

Rory's eyes narrowed incredulously. "You're kidding, right?

Ailis glanced around the room, then leaned closer, speaking some of the things that had been bothering her lately. "Win or lose in this competition, Rory, I think we both know Hunter's going far in the business."

Ailis's fondness for the woman grew even more when she didn't hesitate to agree. "Absolutely. He's phenomenal."

"He has no idea what that lifestyle is like."

The sudden understanding in Rory's eyes told Ailis she'd found a good person to confide in. "You grew up on the road, Ailis. You know the lifestyle takes its toll. Nothing feels real or solid because we're building this city on a stage every night, then tearing it down hours later, taking off and building it somewhere else the next night. It's hard to keep sight of what's real and what's make-believe."

"Is that what happened to you and Eddie?"

Rory nodded slowly. "He loved the lifestyle and I fooled myself into thinking we had something special because we had that in common—the band, the travel, the crazy schedule. I thought we were kindred spirits. Then I found him in bed with three groupies one night."

"Oh. Shit."

Rory laughed. "Yeah, no kidding."

Ailis couldn't help feeling like she wasn't getting the whole story. Rory didn't seem particularly sad about Eddie's unfaithfulness. "So what happened?"

"I took off. The Road Rebels broke up the same day Eddie and I did. Now I'm fighting like hell to fly solo."

"It looks like it's working. Your fan base is growing by the minute."

One of the things Ailis liked most about Rory was her ability to be both self-confident and humble. "Maybe. One minute you're on top in this business and the next you're rock-bottom. I have to admit, sometimes I feel queasy riding these damn waves. I wonder what it would be like to walk out of the ocean and just sit on the shore for a while."

"The shore is nice," Ailis said, recalling her desire to put down roots in Baltimore when she was younger. Now she found herself missing the waves.

"What's worrying you about Hunter, Ailis?" Rory asked.

"I just got out of a long-term relationship with a guy who liked what I could do for him more than he liked me."

"And you think the same thing is true of Hunter?"

Ailis shook her head slowly. "No. I don't."

"You're ahead of the game, Ailis. You're going into this relationship with your eyes wide open, completely aware of what you're facing, both in the lifestyle and with the man. You can guide him through all the bullshit that comes with fame."

"Excuse me," a young woman said as she stepped next to Rory. "Could I have an autograph?"

"Thanks for the talk," Ailis said. "I'll leave you to it."

Rory turned to visit with one of her fans while Ailis quietly slipped away. She joined Hunter and her Pop Pop at the bar, both of them surrounded by lots of regulars of the pub.

The crowd at Pat's Pub, infamous for their love of sports and betting—not necessarily in that order—had been wagering on Hunter's chances of winning since the first show.

Ailis had even placed a bet herself, swearing from day one that he was going to win the whole thing. She'd gotten amazing odds.

Pop Pop lifted his Guinness to her as she sat down.

"So proud of you, my little Ailis. You and Hunter have turned the city on its ear."

She leaned over to kiss her grandfather on the cheek as Hunter said, "Thanks, Mr. Collins."

"No need to be so formal after all this time, son. Call me Pat, or even Pop Pop."

Her grandfather winked at her, making it completely obvious that he preferred the latter. Pop Pop resided on Team Hunter and made no bones about it.

"Hey, Pop," Tris said, tilting his head toward the back of the pub.

"Oh good. They're here. Got a surprise for you, Ailis," Pop Pop said, turning around and gesturing toward the door that led to her apartment.

Her eyes widened when she spotted her parents walking out. "Oh my God!" She grabbed Hunter's hand and pushed her way through the crowd.

"Mom! Dad!" They reached out as she approached, engulfing her in a huge three-person hug. "What are you doing here? I didn't think you were getting back for another week."

Dad lifted her feet a few inches off the ground. Her dad gave the world's greatest bear hugs. "We wanted to surprise you, sweet pea. We came to see the finale of *February Stars*."

Hunter groaned. "Damn. No pressure there."

Ailis laughed. "You two remember Hunter, right?"

Dad shook his hand. "Of course we do. Our paths have passed a few times this year."

Mom and Dad had been home—in Baltimore— more than they'd been away the past decade, but with the pending Universe Reunion tour, that time had grown less in the last year as they embarked on a grueling promotional tour including interviews and scattered engagements throughout the States.

Her mom gestured at an empty table with a reserved sign and they all sat down. Most of the folks in the pub tonight were regulars who'd known Teagan and Sky for years. As such, her parents could usually spend at least an hour or so unmolested before word got out they were in the house and the paparazzi and local fans descended on the place.

Dad thanked Tris for the pint he delivered, then looked at Hunter. "We're looking forward to hearing you sing."

Padraig and Colm approached the table, slapping Hunter on the back. "You're in for a treat, Uncle Sky. Hunter is killer on the guitar," Padraig said, his slurred words alerting Ailis to the fact her cousin was probably already a few pints into the celebration.

"You're going to take the whole competition," Colm added. "Which pains me to say because I stand to lose money."

Hunter laughed. "You bet against me, huh?"

"Didn't have much choice. Ailis wasn't going to, and besides," Colm glanced toward the front of the pub, "that Rory Summit is not hard on the eyes. Or the ears."

Padraig rolled his eyes. "My conservative, stick-in-the-mud bro here is starstruck."

Colm shrugged off the jest good-naturedly. Even though they were identical twins, apart from their looks, there was precious little similar about the brothers. "We're all really excited for you, Hunter. Seriously. You deserve to be in that finale."

"Thanks, guys. I'm not sure it's sunk in yet. I mean..." Hunter's words faded away, drawing Ailis's attention to whatever had caught his eye.

That was when she saw Rhonda standing near the table, looking at Hunter.

She panicked briefly, concerned Paul was with her. While her dad, cousins and uncles were completely lax when it came to Hunter, there was no way her ex-boyfriend was going to venture in here unscathed. Mercifully, Paul was nowhere to be seen.

Padraig and Colm made themselves scarce in the face of the potential scene—not that Ailis fooled herself into thinking they wouldn't hover nearby in hopes of hearing everything.

Rhonda approached the table, never once looking in Ailis's direction. All her attention was focused on Hunter.

"Hi," Rhonda said shyly.

"Hey," Hunter said. Ailis noticed his voice lacked the anger he'd displayed the first time they'd run into their exes. Which meant either his hostility was toward Paul, not both of them, or like her, Hunter had moved on.

"Congratulations," she continued. "I won a ticket at work to see the show last week. I was blown away."

Hunter nodded slowly. "Thanks."

"I was wondering if," Rhonda hesitated and glanced at Ailis for the first time before facing him

190

again, "wondering if I could talk to you alone for a second."

Hunter frowned, clearly unhappy with her request. "Rhonda—"

Ailis saw the dark circles under Rhonda's eyes, and realized she needed to clear the air with Hunter as much as Paul had with her. While Paul's attempt had been fairly lame, it had actually proven to Ailis that she was completely over the guy.

"I think that's a good idea," Ailis said to Hunter. She recalled all the late-night texts she'd taken in Rhonda's stead when he'd been drunk and brokenhearted. The last one had been sent less than five months ago. So yeah. There were things that needed to be said, a chance for both of them to get some of the bad feelings out, so that he could move on once and for all.

Hunter sighed, and Ailis realized he didn't want to talk to his ex-fiancée. "Ailis—"

"Hunter," she repeated, in the same mimicking tone. She winked at him, hoping to prove to him that she wasn't jealous or worried. She trusted him. The fact that Rhonda had braved the lion's den to find him told Ailis she was desperate, and not likely to back off until she'd said her piece.

"Fine," he said at last, rising. "I'll be right back."

Hunter and Rhonda walked toward the front of the pub and Ailis lost sight of them in the crowd.

"You're in love with him," Mom said when Ailis finally turned her attention back to them.

Ailis didn't answer that, still not quite ready. "He's going to be famous."

Dad nodded. "Yeah. I'm pretty sure that's exactly where he's headed, with your help."

"Tour managers travel," she said, not because that bothered her as much as old habits died hard.

Her father chuckled. "Sell that to somebody else, baby girl. White picket fences don't make a home. People do. And you know that."

While her dad saw through her excuse for just what it was—bullshit—her mother took it to heart. "Was your childhood that bad?"

Ailis felt instantly guilty. Mainly because the idea that she'd suffered on the road was so preposterous. While there were parts of the lifestyle she abhorred—paparazzi at the top of the list—there were a million other things that made it wonderful. She'd had the best childhood any kid could have asked for. "Of course not. I didn't mean that. I'm sorry, Mom."

Her mother still looked concerned. "It's not the first time I've heard you say it. I know your upbringing was far from normal, but I always thought—hoped—that it was something you would look back on fondly."

"I do. I swear I do. I wouldn't trade one second of my childhood. Honest. I think my comments were just based on the typical kid philosophy of wanting what I couldn't have. I saw all the aunts and uncles and cousins living here, seeing each other every day, and I thought that was what I wanted. I've had it now for the past ten years and it's great. But it's not better. It's just different."

"You know you can have both," Dad said. "Buy yourselves a house here and set up a travel schedule you can live with. That's what your mom and I ended up doing."

"That's probably what I'm going to do as well. I'm always going to need some Baltimore time. I'm not sure I can go completely cold turkey on the Collins clan. They're too much fun."

"That they are. So your confusion is based on more than traveling for the job," Mom said.

Ailis nodded. "Yeah."

"You're not still hung up on Paul, are you?" Dad asked.

She shook her head. "I'm not hung up on him, but he was sort of the issue."

Mom reached across the table and grasped her hand to hold. "What do you mean?"

"I was invisible in that relationship, a nonentity. And as much as I'd like to blame Paul for that, it wasn't his fault. It was mine. I followed blindly, taking a job at that marketing firm because it was here in Baltimore, which is where Paul wanted to live. I didn't like that job."

Her mom smiled. "I know."

"It's like I couldn't make a move without considering how it impacted him. If it would suit him. This past year, I've been trying to figure out who I am, and I'm struggling. Next thing I know, Hunter is in the picture, and now I'm afraid…"

"You're going to stand in his shadow."

Ailis nodded.

"Take Hunter out of the equation, Ailis. What's your dream job?"

The answer to that was simple. "What I've been doing the past two months. Working with Hunter on his image, his songs, his performances. I didn't realize how much I've missed being in that environment. It energizes me, challenges me. It's fun."

"Even if that means you're facing life on the road again?" Dad asked.

She grimaced. "I played that card because Paul would never have considered traveling with me. Or having a wife who was away from home so often, hanging out with musicians. I said it so many times over those six years he and I were together that I think I started to believe it."

Dad took a sip of her beer. "Les has been waiting for the green light on this, ready to bring you in as a partner in hopes that you'll take over when he retires."

While her dad looked pleased with the turn of events, Mom's expression was pensive. The conversation was about to get a lot harder because her mom never hesitated to ask the really hard questions, a habit Ailis suspected she'd inherited from Pop Pop. "So, we have the work front and living situation settled. Guess it's time for the real question. It sounds to me like you didn't like the person you were when you were with Paul."

Ailis shrugged one shoulder. "Not sure I even classified as a person."

"You and Hunter have been almost inseparable for the last year, isn't that right?"

"Yeah. He's my best friend."

"Why?"

Ailis frowned, searching for the right words. "He makes me laugh. He forces me out of my comfort zone. He says the sweetest things to me and I know they aren't lines. I know he means them. When he looks at me, he sees something special."

"Something worth being seen," Mom said.

Ailis considered that. "Yeah."

"He doesn't sound like the kind of guy who would let a woman hide in the shadows."

"Maybe he wouldn't, but what if I—"

"Ailis," her mom said. "You're one of the smartest people I've ever known. A quick study. And on top of that, you're a lot stronger than you realize. You've learned from your experience with Paul. You've grown. You're too smart to make the same mistake again and too strong to ever let another man run roughshod over you."

Ailis let the words sink in, and she realized she'd been a fool. "I overthink stuff, don't I?"

"Oh God, yeah," Dad muttered. "Took us six car dealerships and eight weeks to buy your first car for you. I thought you'd never pick one."

She laughed. "There were a lot of factors involved in that. Safety, gas mileage, coolness equation, what color to buy."

Mom reached over and wiped a strand of hair away from her eyes. "You've always been careful, Ailis. Very cautious. There's nothing wrong with that. Unfortunately, when it comes to matters of the heart, you have to take a leap of faith. Trust Hunter, but more than that, trust yourself."

"I was really wrong the first time."

Mom shook her head. "Sweetheart, there's not a person on earth who hasn't made a mistake. Think of your time with Paul as a hard-learned lesson. If not for him, you wouldn't appreciate Hunter as much as you do."

"I wouldn't have even found Hunter." Even as she spoke the words, she couldn't imagine a life without Hunter in it. She glanced over her shoulder.

Dad pointed toward the front door of the pub. "He and Rhonda went outside. The fact you encouraged him to walk away with the woman who stole your *last* boyfriend tells me a lot about you and Hunter."

"Oh yeah?" she said with a grin, pleased by her father's approval.

"Yeah. You trust him."

Her mother's words all those years ago drifted back to her.

Trust and love.

She felt both of those things for Hunter.

"Here." He handed Ailis a set of keys. "They're to the bus, which is parked in the lot two blocks down.

Your mom and I are going to drink some whiskey and spend the night upstairs. Why don't you show Hunter what he's letting himself in for if he wins tomorrow night? Probably not fair to let the guy go into it completely blind."

"He hasn't won yet."

"Even if he loses, I don't doubt for a second you're going to move heaven and earth to launch his career. Give him an inside glimpse. Make sure he's ready for it."

It wasn't a bad idea. She and Hunter had been so focused on merely winning the competition, they hadn't discussed what his life would be like if he did. If he walked off that stage tomorrow with a win, his entire life was going to change.

"Okay." She rose and gave her dad a kiss on the cheek. "Thanks, Dad."

Mom stood up and hugged her. "I'm so happy for you," she whispered in Ailis's ear.

Ailis headed for the exit to find Hunter. She'd given Rhonda enough time to say what she wanted to. Now it was Ailis's turn to come clean. She grinned at the thought.

She'd nearly reached the door when Uncle Aaron entered with Les and Hunter. Aaron nodded at her brusquely before heading to Rory.

Les and Hunter came straight to Ailis.

"Where's Rhonda?" she asked.

"Later," Hunter said, looking around the pub anxiously.

She glanced from Hunter to Les, who seemed equally worried. "What's wrong?"

"Not here," Les said, leading the way back to the door to her apartment. She and Hunter followed and when she glanced over her shoulder, she noticed Uncle Aaron and Rory were in route as well.

Once the five of them were alone in the living room of the apartment, Aaron spoke. "How well do the two of you know Robbie Pierson?"

Hunter shrugged. "I met him that night he came here with Rory and the other contestants. The guy's a talented singer, but he's sort of awkward when he's not onstage. Never really establishes eye contact, flinches if someone talks to him."

Ailis added her own opinion to the mix. "Hunter and I talked about him quite a bit one night. We said it's like he has a split personality. He's very calm, cool and collected onstage, a loveable Ed Sheeran type, but offstage, he walks around like a timid puppy."

Rory shook her head at Aaron. "If you've brought us up here to tell us Robbie is the one who's been doing all these things, you're crazy. I've known him for nearly five years, performed more than a few shows with him. That guy couldn't hurt a flea."

Aaron crossed his arms. "Your split personality comment is an interesting one, Ailis. His manager said he was recently diagnosed with schizophrenia."

"His manager told you that?" Ailis asked, surprised the man would reveal something so damning against his client.

Aaron nodded. "Yeah. Robbie disappeared after last week's show. His manager came to the police precinct this morning, concerned that something bad had happened to him. Said they've been working to regulate his medication. The guy seemed to think they had things under control. But then he lost the contest and disappeared."

"You think it was Robbie doing all these things? How? He was at the Soundstage with me and Rory when Ailis was hit by the car," Hunter said.

Les sat down on the couch, sighing heavily. "I talked to his agent a good bit this afternoon. He said

Robbie's got a brother who's sort of bad news. Spent some time in prison for assault. He's out now, but pretty into drugs. Apparently, he's always hitting Robbie up for cash."

"You think he's working with his brother?" Rory asked.

Aaron shrugged. "That's just a theory. We don't have any proof yet. I've got a couple of detectives studying the tape the coffee shop guy provided of your hit-and-run, Ailis. It was grainy as hell, but they've determined the make and model of the car. Originally, we'd hit a brick wall, trying to trace it back to the competitors or their agents. Now, we're looking at the brother." Aaron stopped speaking when his phone rang.

Turning his back, the rest of them listened quietly as he said, "Mmm hmmm. Okay. Yeah. Get the warrant."

When Aaron faced the room again, he looked as if he'd struck gold. "We've got him. The brother rented a car just like the one that struck you two weeks ago. According to the guy at the rental place, there was a dent in the front side panel. And another one of my detectives just got back from the motel where we found the dog."

"Let me guess," Hunter said, "the brother had been staying there."

"Yep. He didn't work too hard to dump the dog. I've got my men issuing warrants to arrest Robbie and his brother."

"So that's it," Rory said. "Mystery solved."

Aaron's expression was solemn as Les shook his head. "This isn't over until Robbie's in custody."

Aaron perched on the coffee table, facing Rory and Hunter. "Les is right. His agent said Robbie took his loss in stride last week, made some comment about being runner-up. Said if anything happened to one of you, he still had a shot."

"His agent thought that was just wishful thinking on Robbie's part," Les continued. "Then more details came out about your hit-and-run, and he became concerned."

Ailis narrowed her eyes. "So concerned he sat on the information he had about Robbie's mental state and disappearance for an entire week?"

Les gave her a grimace. "He's still Robbie's agent. You know how the game's played, kiddo."

Unfortunately, she did.

Aaron looked at Rory. "Where are you staying tonight?"

Rory pointed to Hunter. "His family's hotel. I've been there the whole time."

"Seriously?" Hunter asked, clearly unaware. Ailis wasn't surprised. Hunter had worked precious little at the hotel since the competition began, his aunt and uncle insisting he take his shot at achieving his dreams.

"Yep. Listening to your aunt and uncle and the housekeepers talk about how great you are keeps my competitive spirit strong."

Hunter laughed. "Sounds to me like you're a glutton for punishment."

"I'm putting one of my men outside, to keep an eye on you. Here's my cell number." Aaron handed Rory his card. "If anyone knocks on your door, call me and don't open the door. Text me in the morning when you're ready to go to the Soundstage and I'll make sure you have an escort."

Rory nodded. "Damn. I haven't been nervous in the competition until this second."

Les rested a comforting hand on her shoulder. "It's going to be okay."

Rory pointed toward the stairs that led back down to the pub. "Can I go now?"

Aaron shook his head. "Give me a few minutes to sort these two out and I'll give you a lift back to the hotel. Do you mind waiting at the bar with Tris?"

"Nope. Gives me a chance to hang with that Pop Pop guy. He is totally cool."

Ailis laughed. "Yeah. He is."

Rory left.

"Where are you two spending the night?"

Hunter started to speak, but Ailis beat him to the punch. "Mom and Dad's tour bus."

Hunter looked over at her with surprise. "Since when?"

She dangled the keychain in her hand in front of his face. "Since Dad loaned me the keys."

"Where is it parked?" Aaron asked.

Ailis pointed out the front window. "The lot two blocks that way."

"Okay. I'll park a police car next to it. Get to the bus and stay there until morning. I don't want either one of you going anywhere without a cop standing beside you until this competition is over. Got it?"

Hunter nodded and Les grimaced. "Fucking ache in my gut is back. At this point in the show, I thought things would be easier, not harder."

Aaron slapped Les on the back. "It'll be okay. In twenty-four hours, it'll be done. With any luck, we'll find Robbie way before that."

Les and Aaron walked downstairs.

"Tour bus?"

Ailis grinned. "I thought you might like a little sneak peek of your future."

Hunter's smile faded, replaced by sheer nervousness. "I haven't won yet, A. Rory is the favorite.

She's good. Really good. Honestly, if I had a chance to vote, I'd probably go for her."

Ailis rolled her eyes as she took his hand. "First of all, you're in the finale. You were supposed to be knocked out in week one, so as far as I'm concerned, you've already won. Secondly, your future on a tour bus is not tied to the results of tomorrow's contest. There are lots of ways to make it big in music. *February Stars* is just one. If that doesn't work, we'll try a few hundred more. And finally, what the hell did Rhonda want?"

Hunter chuckled. "Shit. Forgot about her."

Ailis tilted her head in a way that said she had not. "She left Paul. Packed her bags and moved back in with her folks a couple of days ago."

Ailis's eyes widened. "Wow. She beat him to the punch. I kind of like the karmic justice in that."

Hunter feigned a shiver. "You're a cold woman, mouse."

"She came to the pub to tell you that?"

Hunter sighed. "I think you know that wasn't all she wanted."

"Of course not. She wants you back."

"Yeah." Hunter opened his mouth to say more, but she cut him off.

"That's not happening."

Her quick, vehement reply left him speechless for a few seconds, something that was very hard to do. Then he crossed his arms, pretending to be confused. "Why not?"

Ailis flashed him a wholly possessive smile. "You know why."

"Tell me anyway."

She stepped closer to him. "Because I'm yours and you're mine."

She expected her words to make him happy, but instead his forehead creased. "Are you just pretending?"

Ailis flexed up on tiptoe to kiss Hunter on the cheek. Then she reached around his neck and pulled his face lower, so she could whisper in his ear. "Those words were never pretend. They've always been true."

With that, she set his smile free. "I'm head over heels in love with you, mouse."

"Ditto."

He bent his head and gave her the kiss of the century as their breath mingled, their tongues touched, and she soaked up every ounce of warmth in his strong embrace.

"Hunter?" she asked when they parted.

"Yeah?"

"Will you take me home?"

He glanced around the apartment. "You are home."

"You know what I mean."

"I thought we were going to the tour bus for the night."

"It doesn't matter where we go, Hunter. I have a feeling we're going to spend the rest of our lives in a million different places—busses, hotels, apartments. Home for me from this day on is where you are."

Chapter Eleven

Hunter kissed her, long and deep, as they let themselves get lost in each other. She wasn't sure how she could have been afraid of this.

"Come on." They clasped hands and walked together to the bus. Neither of them mentioned the police officer who was following at a polite distance. True to his word, Aaron had parked a cop car right next to the bus. Knowing her overprotective uncle, if he could have found a way, Aaron would have put the car on top of the bus and kept the lights flashing all night as a beacon for Robbie to stay the hell away.

Ailis kept her eyes on Hunter's face as they entered the bus. His response didn't disappoint.

"Holy fuck," he muttered.

She'd grown up on the bus just prior to this one. When they were a family of four roaming around the country, their needs had been different. Once she and her sister had planted their feet on solid ground—Ailis in Baltimore and Fiona in Los Angeles—her parents had downsized on the kid-friendly aspects and upgraded on the luxury.

"Obviously, we won't be riding around in something as posh as this once you start touring, but I figure it gives us something to aim for."

Hunter stopped looking around the bus, his gaze locked with hers. "Say that again."

She frowned, confused. "What?"

"The parts that contained the words *we* and *us*. I like the way they sound."

"So do I," she admitted. Now that her feelings had found their way to the surface, she was hard-pressed not to tell him she loved him over and over again. "When Fiona and I visit, this," she pointed to a couch, "turns into a double bed. All you have to do is push that button."

She continued the tour, enjoying his shocked exclamations as they roamed through the kitchen area, telling stories about learning to cook on a bus. Then they peeked into the bathroom and she discussed some of the epic battles she and Fiona had, fighting for room in that small space. Finally, they wound up in the bedroom. Her parents' king-size bed filled a lot of the space and looked far too inviting.

"This bus is better than most houses I've been in," he said at last.

"Yeah. It really is. But like I said, the band bus isn't this fancy. Or spacious. Or nice. The musicians sleep in narrow bunks, stacked like pancakes. And it takes a while to get used to the constant motion while you're sleeping."

"Did you ever sneak a boy back onto the bus while your parents were performing and make out on their bed?"

She snorted. "Oh my God, no. I was way too big a nerd for that. Fiona did, though. Plenty of times. She was the wild child, not me."

Ailis and Fiona had lived on opposite coasts for nearly a decade, and she still missed her sister as much as if she'd packed her bags and boarded the flight yesterday. Growing up, they only had each other, which basically meant they loved and hated each other with equal amounts of passion.

"Seems like a missed opportunity," he murmured.

She laughed. "Only you would see it that way."

Hunter pushed Ailis down on the bed, caging her under him. "Pretty sure everyone would see it that way."

As was becoming Hunter's standard operating procedure, whenever he thought a conversation was over, he put a period at the end with a kiss.

Ailis loved the weight of his body on top of hers, the way he sheltered her completely, making her feel safe and warm and cherished. It was a unique sensation, something she'd never experienced with Paul. For a second, she tried to puzzle out what the difference was, but then Hunter deepened the kiss and she realized.

She hadn't ever truly loved Paul. She thought she had, but she hadn't had enough experience with the emotion to know she was wrong.

Hunter lifted her shirt, his tongue teasing the tops of her breasts along the edge of her bra. Then he sucked one of the nipples into his mouth, lace and all. It was strangely erotic, hotter this way. He turned his head and treated the other to the same.

Ailis ran her fingers through his auburn hair. "We're both gingers."

He lifted his head and grinned at her. "You're just noticing that?"

"It occurs to me that if we ever have kids, they won't stand a chance."

Hunter's responses never failed to surprise her. She'd been making a joke, but his gaze went serious. "Not if. When. I want kids with you, Ailis. A whole bus full of them."

She giggled. "Trust me. Two kids in a bus will feel like a hundred." She bit her lower lip nervously, recalling the times she'd made these same plans, dreamed these same dreams with Paul. "Kind of early in the relationship to start planning marriage and kids and stuff like that. I mean, this is sort of like five minutes old."

He shook his head. "I'm not him, A. I don't say things I don't mean."

Her brow creased. The man read her like a damn book. "I know you don't. Which is why I feel compelled to reiterate that it won't be a bus full."

Hunter laughed loudly before pressing his lips against her stomach, kissing it reverently. She could imagine him doing the same thing when she was pregnant. Kissing their baby. Hunter would be an amazing dad. Probably a lot like hers.

When he looked up again, his face reflected pure mischief. "We're going to right a wrong, mouse."

"Ooookay," she drawled, wondering what he was talking about.

"Tonight, you're going to be the wild child." He stood up and flipped on some music, searching until he found one of her parents' albums. He adjusted the volume, then glanced over his shoulder as if looking for someone coming. Facing her again, she marveled at how he seemed to change, his expression almost nervous. "How much longer is this concert going to last? Don't want your folks walking in on us."

She smiled, falling into the role without hesitation. She listened to the music for a second, pretending to consider his question. "They have five more songs in this set. Then they'll do two encores."

Hunter tugged his T-shirt over his head. "Then we'll have to be quick."

Ailis quickly amended her dialogue. "Actually, we probably have more time than you think. I bet they'll do four encores. It's a great crowd tonight."

He chuckled. "How much trouble will you get into if your dad catches us?"

She sat up on the bed and pulled her shirt off, loving the way his eyes drifted to her breasts and lingered appreciatively.

Ailis adopted a shy, uncertain voice, realizing the role wasn't much of a stretch for her. "I'm sort of surprised you left the concert to be with me instead of Rory. She's gorgeous."

Hunter shrugged, unimpressed. "Rory's not you. Pretty sure I couldn't pick her out of a lineup right now."

Ailis laughed. "Liar," she whispered.

"Will you take your bra off too? I understand if you don't want to, it's just..."

She was used to Hunter being confident in the bedroom, taking charge, driving her wild. But there was something endearingly sexy about this Hunter too. She bet he broke a million hearts back in high school with that charming, earnest smile.

"Okay," she said. She reached behind her to unclasp the bra, heat rushing to her cheeks. The role-play suddenly felt too real. While it had never happened, it was easy to imagine her parents onstage singing while she snuck away with a boy to make out. God knew Fiona had done that enough times to make up for Ailis's eternal goody-two-shoes lifestyle.

When Hunter sat next to her on the bed and cupped her cheek, her life was upended. She'd always thought herself the smart one, her sister the fun one. Fiona had clearly been the smarter one. Because fun was way better.

"You're blushing."

She lowered her face, trying to shield the damning color with her hair. Hunter tilted her face up, refusing to let her hide.

"I like it. You're so pretty, Ailis."

He leaned closer to kiss her, but unlike his earlier ones, this one was softer, more innocent, almost exploratory. The man was one hell of a role player.

She wasn't sure, but she thought his fingers might have trembled a little when he reached out tentatively to touch one of her breasts.

Ailis pulled away from the kiss to suck in some much-needed air. She actually felt nervous. As if this was the first time she'd ever gotten to second. "Hunter," she whispered.

"I just want to touch you, Ailis. I swear I won't go any further than that. Just touch."

"Okay."

His fingers were still too gentle. Ailis wrapped her arms around his waist, pressing her own innocent kisses to his chest. She kept her face pressed against him so he couldn't see her when she made her request. "Harder. Squeeze them harder."

Hunter complied, then dropped character for just a moment when he pinched one of her nipples tightly. She groaned, then mimicked his rougher touch by biting his nipple.

He jerked away, surprised by her action. "Wild child," he murmured. "Will you take off your jeans? I won't put it in if you don't want me to."

Ailis unfastened her jeans, tugging the denim and her panties off. She was completely naked, while Hunter had only lost his shirt. The shyness she'd worn around for so many years fell away too. His words had taken root. She did feel wild, reckless.

Rising, she twisted on the bed, straddling his lap. Hunter's hands flew to her waist when she bent her head and kissed him. Hard.

With the element of surprise on her side, she pushed him to his back on the bed, following him down, refusing to give up on the passionate kiss. Hunter's hands roamed over her back, pulling her flush against him, her breasts crushed against his hard abs.

She cradled his erection, covered by his jeans, against her opening. Unable to resist, she began to rub herself against his crotch, seeking stimulation.

Through it all, they kissed. One of Hunter's hands rose to her hair, twisting the strands around his fingers and using his grip to hold her where he wanted her.

Ailis ran her fingernails along his sides, enjoying the shudder her scratches evoked.

"Goddammit," Hunter grunted, when he used his grip on her hair to tug her away. "You're playing with fire, little girl."

She gave him a seductive grin that told him his warning had fallen short. "Seems to me you're the one who's in over his head."

All pretense fell away as Hunter—her Hunter—returned in full dominant fashion. He rolled them both in one swift motion that put him back on top. He rested on his elbows, his face inches from hers as he pressed his covered cock against her clit harder.

"You sure you can handle that?" he taunted.

Rather than respond, she lifted her head. And bit his shoulder.

That appeared to be the only answer he needed. He shoved away from her for the eternal twenty seconds it took for him to kick off his shoes and shed his jeans. Rather than resume his place above her, he gripped her ankles and tugged her ass to the edge of the bed. He knelt on the floor, placed her legs over his shoulders, then gave her a much better brand of French kiss.

She wasn't the only one who'd been stripped bare of control. Primal was a much better word for how she felt. Eager. Grasping. Clawing.

Hunter nipped at her clit before applying a powerful stroke with his tongue as he drove two fingers inside of her. Her back arched.

"Finally," she growled, her fingers gripping his hair, holding him to her pussy as if he were her very own concubine.

Two fingers became three and Hunter moved faster, sucking harder on her clit.

Stars erupted as she screamed, coming with the force of a freight train.

Hunter ignored her climax, continuing to finger fuck her as if it had never happened. Her body didn't have time to recover, to adjust. In the past, she'd been a one-and-done girl, but Hunter didn't play that way.

"Hunter," she protested.

"Do it again," he demanded.

"I—" She was on the verge of telling him she couldn't, but the words never made land. They couldn't because the second orgasm took her down even harder. "Holy. Fuck!"

She trembled, the pleasure of it so intense, it sort of fucking hurt. "God," she gasped.

Now, like before, Hunter seemed oblivious to her response as he cranked up the sexual torment. He drew his wet fingers out of her pussy, so that he could use her body's juices to press one thick digit into her ass. Three thrusts—two shallow and then the one that lodged it deep.

Her breath was ragged and so loud it was drowning out the music. Her gaze found Hunter's. His name suited him at the moment. He'd stalked his prey and now, the all-powerful hunter was going in for the kill. The finger in her ass started thrusting at the exact same time he drove the thumb of his other hand into her pussy. She was doubly penetrated and her nerves were too sensitive from the first two climaxes.

When he bent his head once more and sucked her clit into his mouth, she erupted like a volcano before things went gray.

Ailis wasn't sure how long she'd been out of it, but when she opened her eyes, Hunter was above her once more.

"There she is."

"What the fuck was that?" she whispered.

Hunter chuckled. "Foreplay."

If she'd had an ounce of strength in her body, she would have laughed. But in truth, his words also provoked a fair amount of panic. "There's no way I can take any more of—"

Hunter cut her off. Not with a kiss, as she was accustomed to. But with something that packed a much bigger punch.

He thrust inside her in one hard shove, his cock buried to the hilt. Her inner muscles quivered at the invasion.

"Fuck," she grunted. "Seriously, Hunter—"

He retreated, halting her complaint with another rough thrust.

This time, her body adjusted, softened. Responded.

Hunter sensed the change, because he stopped giving her time in between each retreat and return. Instead, he took her the way she'd always fantasized about in her raciest daydreams. He fucked her like she mattered, like she was sex and passion and love and everything he needed in the world.

It was beautiful. Perfect.

He paused for a second, his eyes narrowed with concern. "Jesus. Am I hurting you?"

She was surprised by his question...until he reached up to wipe away a tear.

"Oh my God, no. Not even close."

He didn't seem to believe her and he rose, pulling out as he went.

"No." She panicked, rising, desperate to drag him back inside. "Please. I mean it."

His gaze raked her body, landing on the damn bruise from the hit-and-run. "Ailis," he started.

"You're not hurting me. I'm not crying because I'm in pain. I'm crying because every single dream I've ever had just came true. In case you're wondering, that's kind of an earth-shattering moment in a woman's life."

He bent his head, his chin falling to his chest so that she couldn't see his face. Then his shoulders started shaking, and she realized he was laughing.

She narrowed her eyes angrily. "Seriously? You're laughing."

Hunter set loose the sound he'd been trying to hold back, howling with mirth, and her temper spiked even more.

"Unbelievable!" She started to climb out of the bed, but he grasped her waist, halting her escape.

"Hey. If you get to cry when you come to that realization, then I'm allowed to laugh when I come to the same one."

She froze, trying to make sense of his words. It sounded like...

"I'm your dream come true?" she asked.

He shook his head. "No, I wasn't smart enough or brave enough to dream up anything as perfect as you, mouse."

"I feel like you should be writing this down."

"What?"

"Do you know what those words would sound like in a song?"

Hunter started laughing again. "Ever the manager. Do you mind if we finish where we left off before I start composing you symphonies?"

"I'll wait." Ailis reached out, pulling him over her body once more, her thighs parted, ready to welcome him back.

He slid in easily, but the entire tenor changed. They both recognized the importance of the moment. Hunter made love to her, kissing her, caressing her, cherishing her.

Ailis ran her hands over every part of his body she could reach, wanting to ensure he knew she loved him. Now. And forever.

Chapter Twelve

Hunter woke up just before dawn to the sound of a gunshot.

Ailis sat straight up, and Hunter panicked as another shot was fired, crashing through a window near the front of the bus.

"Oh my God!" Ailis cried out.

He pushed her down on the mattress, covering her as a third bullet struck the bus, closer this time. She shivered beneath him, struggling a bit.

"The floor," she gasped. "We should get on the floor."

Before he could respond, the siren of the police cruiser parked next to them pierced what had been a quiet morning. The cop car peeled tires and took off after…something. Hunter was blind to what was happening. Helpless.

Ailis lay beneath him, her breath coming in rapid, panic-stricken gasps.

Everything outside went quiet again.

The whole episode had lasted less than thirty seconds, yet Hunter felt as if he'd lived a thousand lifetimes in that span.

"Do you think it's over?" Ailis whispered.

Hunter didn't move, refusing to leave her unprotected. "I don't know."

She tried to push up, but he wouldn't give way. They were still in her parents' bed, completely naked. They'd fallen asleep last night after making love. Funny how the most perfect night in history could end in the world's most terrifying morning. "No, mouse. Lay still." He reached over for his cell and called Aaron's number.

"Hunter, are you and Ailis alright?" Aaron yelled through the phone by way of greeting.

"Yeah. Somebody fired off a few shots at the bus."

"I know. I just heard it come across the wire. The cop I had posted outside is in pursuit. Bullets were fired from a car driving by. Same vehicle fired shots at Rory's hotel window. My guy was stationed in the foyer and by the time he got to his car and started pursuit, the vehicle was gone. We didn't realize it was headed straight for you."

"Is Rory okay?"

"Rory!" Ailis shoved hard until Hunter had no choice but to let her sit up.

"She's fine," Aaron said, as Hunter put him on speakerphone. "Wild shots. Fired by a desperate man."

"Or men," Ailis corrected.

"Either way, the police protection must have thrown them. Listen, I need to get to the station. Stay put. I've got another officer coming to take you both back to the pub."

"No," Ailis said. "I don't want to put the family in danger. We'll go back to Hunter's, bunker down there."

"Okay. I'll be in touch." Aaron disconnected before they could say goodbye.

"We better get dressed," she said, rising from the bed. Hunter watched her try to pull her shirt on with trembling hands and reached out to help her.

"Let me," he said, aware that his hands weren't exactly steady either. Together, they managed to get their clothes on and the bed made.

"I guess we should go check out the damage up front while we wait for the police officer."

Ailis blew out an unsteady breath. "Yeah."

Hunter led the way, shaking his head as they traversed the narrow hallway. "It's not worth all this," he muttered. "It's just a contest."

"Maybe to you."

Ailis screamed as Robbie stepped into view, his gun trained directly at Hunter's chest.

Hunter glanced toward the door of the bus. They hadn't been firing shots wildly. They'd hit what they were aiming for. With the glass of the door broken, it had been easy for Robbie to push his way through it.

"Where's your brother?" Hunter asked.

His question didn't appear to take Robbie by surprise, which proved the other man knew the jig was up.

"High-speed police chase. He was just a diversion."

"Obviously. But you have to know the cops are on to you," Hunter said, silently praying he played this the right way. It was hard to know what would cause Robbie to pull that trigger. Right now, Hunter's number one priority was keeping the man talking and keeping Ailis behind him and safe until the cops got here.

"Ten years," Robbie muttered, waving the gun around. "Been performing for ten fucking years. And you know what I have to show for it?"

Hunter shook his head slowly.

"*Nothing.* That's what. Everyone is conspiring against me. I know. I've heard everyone talking about me, my career, working to keep me down."

Hunter was fairly certain "everyone" in this scenario were the voices in Robbie's head. "That's not true, man. You were picked to compete in this show because you've got real talent. How many performers would have killed for a slot? And you got it. Because you've got what it takes. Hell, you came in third. That's incredible. Do you know how many recording studios are probably looking at you right now? Planning their deals, calling your agent."

Robbie's eyes didn't even brighten at the prospect. He looked out of it, maybe even stoned. "That's not true. You're lying. They told me you were a liar. That you'd do whatever it took to win. You're fucking *her* just to get to her parents. To get..." Robbie's eyes began to scan the bus as if he'd only just realized where he was. "To get here."

Hunter wanted to refute Robbie's accusations, but the guy was seriously unsteady and he didn't want to do anything to piss him off, to make him pull that trigger. If it was just him on the bus, maybe he'd take a chance and jump him, but right now, all Hunter could think about was getting Ailis out alive. This asshole had nearly killed her once. He wasn't getting another shot as long as there was breath in Hunter's body.

So he took a different path. "You're right, Robbie. I've been taking the easy way, using Ailis. I knew I couldn't get in the contest on my own, figured she could get me there and she did."

He felt Ailis's hand on his back.

"Didn't realize," Hunter continued, "she's got fuck all to do with the contest. She can't help me win like I thought. She's useless. Tell you what, why don't you let her go and you and me can sit down and set things straight. I'll call Les and tell him I'm bailing on the show. You're the one who should have been in the finale all along. Let's get Ailis out of the way and we'll make it happen."

"I'm not leaving," she whispered, low enough that Hunter was certain Robbie hadn't heard. Hell, he wasn't sure Robbie heard anything. His eyes were still roaming around the bus.

He glanced at her over his shoulder, but didn't move his body, careful to keep her completely shielded from the weapon aimed their way.

"Sorry, mouse," he said, evoking as much disdain as he could into the nickname. "It's been fun, but I'm afraid I don't have any more use for you."

Her eyes narrowed angrily.

Please God, let her forgive me for this.

"Why don't you leave and let me and Robbie handle this?"

"She's not going anywhere!" Robbie yelled, his attention back on them. "Neither one of you are."

In the distance, through the front windshield of the bus, Hunter could see the lights of a police car, heading their direction, just a few blocks away. As agitated as Robbie was, it was obvious all hell was about to break loose.

Hunter looked around at where they were standing. He was next to the dining table. If he timed it right, if he managed to use the element of surprise against Robbie, there was a good chance he could shove Ailis under it before a shot was fired. Unfortunately, he was pretty sure he'd only have time to save her. Meanwhile, he was stuck out in the open, with nothing to hide behind and too far away to charge the man.

Ailis's hand left his back and Hunter worried about what she was doing, but he didn't dare turn to look at her. He was counting the seconds until Robbie realized the cops were there.

"You're both to blame for this!" Robbie was screaming now, and they were hitting critical mass. "You and that bitch, Rory. She's next. That bitch is next!"

Those were the last words Robbie spoke.

At that point, Hunter went into shock as he watched events unfold. Terror overtook him and the only noise he could hear was his heartbeat pounding in his ears.

Robbie's last word still hovered in the air as the police car squealed to a halt next to the bus.

Hunter saw his moment as Robbie's head whipped to the left.

But Ailis saw it first.

She shoved him down by launching herself onto his back, even as something whizzed by his head.

The frying pan she'd thrown struck Robbie soundly on the forehead. The man flew back and his hand rose up involuntarily. He fired, but the bullet went skyward.

The cop was out of the car, firing in the open door at Robbie before he could get another round off.

Three shots later and Robbie was lying on the floor of the bus. Dead.

Hunter had watched it all happen from the floor of the bus in the five seconds after Ailis had tackled him. It had felt like twelve lifetimes. They lay still, neither of them moving, until the cop flew up the steps of the bus.

"Are you two okay?"

Hunter nodded. "Yeah. Yeah. It's okay. It's okay." He'd become a parrot, everything coming out twice.

The cop glanced down at Robbie's lifeless body and picked up the other man's weapon. "I'll take care of this and radio for an ambulance." He left the bus and returned to his car.

That's when Hunter's brain reengaged. He rose up from the floor, standing as Ailis slid down his back, finding her own feet.

He twisted around, more furious than he'd ever been in his life. "What the fuck did you just do?" he bellowed.

"What?" she scowled, clearly confused by his sudden anger.

"You could've been killed! What the fuck were you thinking?"

She put her hands on her hips and when she spoke again, her fury matched his. "I thought I was saving our lives!"

"I had a plan!"

"What plan?"

He pointed to the table. "I was going to shove you under there."

She rolled her eyes, backing up the mocking expression with a loud, "Ha! Yeah, that would've worked. What about you and the gun that asshole was pointing at you? He would have *shot* you."

"I'm aware of that, but dammit, Ailis, what you did wasn't any better. All you did was ensure *you* were in the line of fire, not me!"

"Right," she said, her voice much quieter, proving that had been her intention.

He shook his head. "No."

"So you get to risk your life for me, but I'm not allowed to do the same? You know what that's called?"

"Chivalry?"

"Sexism."

He threw his hands up, exasperated. "Oh, for fuck's sake. Are you seriously accusing me of sexism for wanting to save your life?"

"All I'm saying—" she started before their conversation was cut off by another voice in the bus.

"Wow. Experiencing some serious déjà vu." Aaron stepped onto the bus and over Robbie's body.

"What?" Ailis asked.

"Riley and I fight about stupid shit like this all the time too. Ask her about the time we walked into a dangerous redneck dive called Jacko's in Vegas back before we were married."

"It's not stupid, Aaron. She threw herself in harm's way."

Aaron shrugged. "Classic female Collins trait. If you're going to stick with this family, Hunter, you need to learn to anticipate their reactions."

Hunter grinned, liking the sound of being invited to stick with the Collins family. "Okay. Right."

Aaron gripped his shoulder. "And just so you know, they're all crazy as hell and you'll never guess right."

Ailis crossed her arms haughtily. "Are you two finished?"

Aaron chuckled. "Yeah. I'm good. We arrested the brother a few miles out of the city on I-95. Your parents are going out of their minds with worry, Ailis. Come back to pub while we," he glanced at the body behind him, "clean up. I'll be along in about an hour or so. Have some routine questions I need to ask."

"Okay," Hunter said, taking Ailis's hand. She squeezed it tightly as they stepped over Robbie's body. Once they were out on the street, he noticed the tears in her eyes. He tugged her close, so grateful to be able to hold her, to know she was safe, unharmed.

Ailis sniffled, then she stopped trying to fight it and cried.

He just clung to her, holding back a few tears of his own. It had been one hell of a week, a roller coaster of emotions.

They were forced to part when the paparazzi arrived. He'd become a celebrity thanks to *February*

Stars, and with each successive week that found him still in the competition, the cameramen flanking him grew.

They quickly walked to Pat's Pub, neither of them speaking or acknowledging the cameras flashing around them.

Ailis's grandfather appeared to possess magic pixie dust, because the paparazzi didn't dare to seek admittance to the pub. Hell, they didn't even cross to the same side of the street. Instead, they set up camp from a distance.

"Between Aaron, Pop Pop, Ewan and Tris, the paparazzi have learned the safe boundaries," Ailis said, answering a question he hadn't asked.

"I wondered."

The rest of the morning was spent surrounded by Ailis's family. Hunter had grown up in a very small family of three, first with his parents and then, after their deaths, with his aunt and uncle. It had been a quiet, safe upbringing, and Hunter had never failed to feel loved. However, those feelings were miniscule in comparison to what the Collins family brought to the table. Every aunt, uncle and cousin within driving distance had arrived to make sure he and Ailis were okay. And the ones who lived too far away had phoned. Fiona had called twice.

Shortly after noon, Ailis managed to extract them both from the crowd, claiming there was still a competition to win.

That might have been a good thing if his afternoon hadn't been as crazy as his morning, between practices, interviews, and sound checks.

Of course, none of that held a candle to the moment that really mattered. The one that came right after he'd given his best performance ever.

He stood under the stifling hot lights for the fourth time in one month, staring at the one X marking the spot for the winner, shoulder to shoulder with Rory. She'd had an equally trying day that started with gunshots.

They'd joked just before the show began that no one could claim the contest hadn't been completely fair. Equal amounts of life and death scares.

"And the winner of *February Stars*..." Mike paused for dramatic effect. "By only twelve votes..." Another pause. The crowd had been silent, which made their collective gasp at how close the results were very obvious. "The performer who is going to open for The Universe on their worldwide tour is..."

Hunter felt like throwing up. He'd performed his ass off on that stage, sung and played the guitar and worked the space and gave out a million of those charming grins Ailis swore would win him votes.

But so had Rory. She'd been magic.

"Rory Summit!" Mike yelled into the microphone as everyone in the place went crazy, applauding, screaming, crying. The Rory fans were jubilant, the Hunter fans sobbing. It was madness.

Hunter turned and hugged Rory. If he had to lose, he was glad it was to her. She'd put in her time and deserved to climb on that tour bus.

"Hunter," she started. "I'm so sor—"

He shook his head and gave her a big smile. "You're a superstar, Rory. And I'm your biggest fan."

While she came across as a tough-as-nails chick, he knew she was marshmallow inside when she wiped away a tear. "Damn you," she muttered as he laughed. She didn't like that he'd made her cry.

"Go sing an encore." Hunter gave the crowd once last wave, directed everyone's attention to their winner, and then left the stage.

He'd purposely avoided looking at Ailis since Mike had called out Rory's name. He'd been too afraid of what he'd see in her face. Devastation? Disappointment?

Taking a deep breath, he glanced up and found her.

She was smiling at him and her face shone with pure pride.

He shrugged. "I lost."

Ailis laughed. "Yeah, I heard that."

"You seem really happy about it."

She rolled her eyes. "Of course I'm not happy about the loss, but I meant what I said last night. You already won." As if she'd timed it, her cell phone rang. She glanced at the screen, then held it up for him to see. "SunTrust Records. They're the fourth recording studio to call me tonight. That's in addition to seven booking agents, three talk shows—including *Ellen*; you are *so* doing that one—and a guy from the Orioles who wants you to throw out the first pitch at their Fourth of July game. *February Stars* was an internet sensation and Les is already talking about making it an annual event."

"You got all those calls today?"

She nodded.

"Why didn't you tell me?"

Ailis lifted one shoulder, looking far too at home in her role as manager. Jesus, for a second he thought she actually resembled Les. A veritable mini-me. Which was disturbing.

"Because I wanted your head in the competition. All you needed to focus on tonight was the show."

"Still lost," he muttered, though the sting of that was wearing off really quick.

"Somebody very wise once told me that life was about winning *and* losing, not one or the other."

Hunter recalled that conversation. "Wise, huh?"

The two of them turned toward the stage as the crowd's volume tripled toward the end of Rory's encore.

"God. They always know how to time an entrance," Ailis said as her parents joined Rory onstage to sing.

And then, Rory surprised him by turning and gesturing for him to join them. He looked at Ailis for approval and she was already nodding enthusiastically. Even so, he hesitated. It felt like this was meant to be Rory's moment. At least until Les thrust a microphone in his hand and shoved him onstage.

He hadn't thought it humanly possible for the already frenetic crowd to get louder, but they did. Hunter stepped next to Rory as Teagan and Sky flanked him and they sang the chorus together, and he knew he was living the number two best moment of his entire life.

Number one was the night he'd walked into his apartment and found the Dear John letter that led him across town to Ailis.

The four of them sang "Maybe Tomorrow" together, much to the fans' delight, and then he, Sky and Teagan left Rory alone to sing just one last encore.

Best night ever.

And it only got better when Ailis took his hand and said, "Let's go celebrate at the pub. I owe Colm some money. Dammit."

He laughed and they all rode together. Rory stayed behind with Les as reporters lined up to interview her.

Several hours later, Hunter and Ailis sat at the bar, surrounded by friends and family. There'd been a million toasts already, and Hunter suspected there would be a million more before this group settled down.

When cheers erupted, he glanced toward the entrance to discover Rory had entered. He grinned and started to order her a pint, but realized something was off. Ailis had clearly noticed too, because she was already off her stool and three steps toward the woman.

Rory gave them a weak smile. "Hey, guys, would you mind coming outside with me a minute? I need to talk to you."

"What's wrong?" Ailis asked.

Rory didn't reply, just turned and led them outside. They walked a few blocks away from the bustling pub toward the waterfront. They didn't ask any questions until they were all three standing at the railing, looking at the harbor.

"Rory—" Hunter started.

"I'm conceding," she said quietly.

"What?" Hunter asked. "*No*. Hell no."

She turned to face him, her expression determined. "My sister collapsed earlier today. She was in ICU until," Rory swallowed heavily, "a few hours ago…"

Ailis reached out and took Rory's hand. "Say it."

"She died."

Ailis winced, squeezing her eyes closed tightly, unable to hold back the tears for a woman she'd never known.

Hunter was struck by the difference between her and Rory, who was completely dry-eyed. Numb.

"She has a four-year-old daughter. My niece, Angel. The love of my life."

"Do you have other family?" Hunter asked.

She shook her head. "Our folks were older parents. They died within a year of each other when my sister and I were in our early twenties."

Suddenly Hunter understood why he'd felt such a kinship with this woman. They were both orphans.

"It's not unheard of to take a child on the road. I grew up that way and it was a wonderful adventure," Ailis said.

Rory refused to consider it. "No. She's just had her life toppled over. I'm not dragging her out of the world she knows and thrusting her into my crazy existence. I've already talked to Les. He knows. He's working up a press release right now and I'm leaving Baltimore tonight. I need to be," her voice cracked, revealing the only chink in her tough armor, "with Angel."

Ailis reached out, hugging Rory tightly, not bothering to stem her own tears. "She's lucky to have you for an aunt," she said thickly.

Rory smiled though her face reflected disbelief. "I hope so. I don't know anything about kids."

Hunter hugged her next. Though they'd only met a month or so ago, he'd become very fond of her. "We're gonna meet again on that stage one day, Rory."

She laughed quietly. "I'd like that. A lot." And with that, she gave them one last sad smile and walked away.

Ailis sniffled quietly as she turned to look at the water.

He put his arm around her shoulder. "Sure as fuck didn't want to win that way."

A soft sob fell from her lips and she turned as he hugged her. "I know. Talk about winning *and* losing. Poor Rory just hit both extremes in a matter of hours."

"She's going to be okay. She's tough, determined, a fighter."

"Yeah. I just can't help but think life sucks sometimes."

Hunter tightened his grip. "It does. It really does."

They were quiet for several minutes, each lost in their thoughts. He placed a soft kiss on top of her head.

"That was a whirlwind day," Hunter said at last. "Not sure we could have crammed in many more highs and lows."

She looked up at him, nodding. "I'm sort of numb."

"Yeah." He cupped her cheek affectionately, wiping away the tracks left behind from her tears.

"Hunter?"

"Yeah, mouse."

"I don't want to feel numb anymore. Spent too many years of my life just existing. I want to come to life. With you."

Hunter took her hand and led her back to the street. They walked in silence to his car and neither of them sought to break the solitude of the moment.

When they entered his apartment, he locked the door and he pushed her against it as every emotion of the day simmered beneath the surface, threatening to consume him.

Ailis reached out for him, kissing him, gripping his shirt. He deepened the kiss, pushing his tongue into her mouth. She nipped at his lower lip, drawing blood.

"Ailis," he warned.

She shook him off, refusing to hear what he had to say. Instead, she reached down, grasped the edges of his shirt and pulled it roughly, tearing the fabric and ripping the buttons off.

"Like that, is it?" he asked with a wolfish grin. He didn't give her a chance to respond. He wrapped his fist in her long red hair and tugged until she gasped. The pleasure-pain had the desired effect. Her eyes went heavy with need.

"Pull harder."

He complied, thrilled at the reaction his rough touch evoked.

Ailis began tackling the button and zipper on his jeans. He let her go until the denim was open—God knew his hard cock needed the room—but then he shoved her hands away.

"Hunter," she complained, trying to reach inside his pants.

"Bad girl," he said, gripping her wrist in an implacable hold as he dragged her to his bedroom.

"Take off your clothes," he demanded as soon as they entered.

She wasted no time, more than ready to take this to the next level. She had no idea what she was rushing toward.

Even in the dim lighting, he could make out the fading, yellowish bruises from the hit-and-run.

He resisted the urge to wince every time he saw them. Ailis swore they weren't sore any longer and he believed her, but that didn't help calm his anger, his fears, as he was reminded once more that she could have been killed. Over *his* dreams.

She caught the direction of his gaze and waggled her finger at him as if he were a naughty boy. "If you go there tonight, I'll have to punish you."

The alpha male in him had just enough pride that her taunt tweaked. "You may run the show when it comes to my career, Ailis, but you're never going to be in charge in the bedroom."

She snorted. "Never is a long time, Hunter."

"Not that long," he muttered as he pressed her back until she fell onto the mattress. He shifted her body until she was in the middle of the bed and pushed inside her without preamble. She was wet and ready for him.

"No foreplay?" she teased.

"I wish I had the patience tonight."

Ailis cupped his cheek. "I'm glad you don't. I feel...I need..."

He kissed her. "I know, mouse. Me too."

They came together in a rush, taking and giving, then demanding more. When he sensed she was close, he reached down to stroke her clit, the touch providing just what she needed. Her orgasm struck only seconds before his. Just another way the two of them were in perfect unison. She was the harmony to his melody.

"I love you, mouse" he whispered once the sensual storm had passed.

Ailis smiled. "I love you too."

Epilogue

Pop Pop was kicked back in his comfy chair when Ailis arrived. The tour was winding down after nine months of nonstop movement, and she'd decided to grab a quick weekend at home in Baltimore. Hunter had planned to come along, but at the last minute, he'd grabbed a slot on *The Tonight Show*. As such, the bus had dropped her off before heading on north. He'd return tomorrow, and they'd spend one night in the dorm before moving on again.

"Hey, Pop Pop," she said as she entered.

He stood, a little more slowly than he would have a couple of years ago, but that didn't matter when he wrapped her up in his seriously strong embrace.

"There's my girl. Where's Hunter?"

"New York for the night. But he'll be back tomorrow and he's hoping the two of you can grab a Guinness at the pub for old time's sake."

"Well now, lass, have you ever known me to turn down an offer of a pint?"

She laughed. "Never."

"Sit down here with me and tell me all about the tour."

Ailis grabbed the chair next to him and spent the better part of an hour telling him all the places they'd been, while sharing funny stories of life on the road that she knew he would embellish and retell his cronies at the pub.

Occasionally, Pop Pop managed to get a word in or ask a question. It took her a while to realize she was worse than a damn telemarketer, and she grinned guiltily.

"Sorry," she said.

"Never apologize for sharing your happiness, Ailis. I must admit, you're a sight for these sore old eyes."

She started to tell another story, but her gaze landed on Pop Pop's wall of photographs. For as long as she could remember, her frame had held a picture of her taken in the library her junior year of college. Pop Pop had latched on to and refused to change it because he said it captured her essence. And for so many years, it had. It revealed an intelligent, serious, quiet, thoughtful...mouse. She'd always thought she looked pretty in it, and she'd taken Pop Pop's comment about her essence as a compliment.

But now... She stood up and walked closer.

"Where did you get this picture?" she asked, leaning forward to study the photograph. It was a fun one of her and Hunter standing together outside the pub. They were wrapped up in coats and she was curled up behind him, hugging him as he looked over his shoulder at her as if she hung the moon.

"Riley snapped it with her phone a few days after Hunter made it to the third round of *February Stars*. Really captures the two of you, doesn't it?"

It did. It revealed best friends in the beginning phases of falling madly in love with each other. And the coolest part was, Ailis suspected if Aunt Riley snapped another picture of them tomorrow, it would still look the same.

No, it would look better. Because the girl in this photo hadn't allowed herself to believe in love and trust and happiness and forever. She knew better now.

"I love it," she whispered.

"Aye, my lovely Ailis, you finally pulled the veil away, revealed your beauty to the world."

Ailis recalled the story her Pop Pop used to tell her when she was just a little girl. She'd always thought it was a prelude to peek-a-boo and the two of them would play as she giggled.

"You know, I looked that story up online once. In the version I read, she was a witch and she wore the veil so people wouldn't die at the sight of her."

Pop Pop chuckled. "Creative license. Story like that would scare a little girl. Besides, it was the moral I was trying to get you to see. You were such a shy little thing, hiding behind your mother."

She rolled her eyes. "Pop Pop. I was four."

Her grandfather didn't reply. Instead, he gave her that look that told her he could wait all day if necessary until she said what he was waiting to hear.

"Fine. The moral wasn't lost on me."

He winked. "Glad to hear it. Though I have to say, it took you a while."

Ailis walked over and kissed him on the cheek. "It took me way too long to figure out who I was, who I wanted to be."

"Given you just talked my fool ear off about everything you and Hunter have been getting into, I think it's safe to say you've found your place in the world."

"I have," she said. "Actually, I didn't just come home for a visit. I wanted to..." She lifted the engagement ring Hunter had given her last weekend.

"Well, look at that." Pop Pop held her hand as he looked at her ring. It was a freaking rock and a half, and she told Hunter he'd lost his mind when he proposed— after she'd put it on her finger, said yes and cried a few minutes. When Pop Pop glanced at her again, there were tears in his eyes. "I'm so happy for you, sweet girl. Feel so damn blessed every day I'm still here to watch you kids grow into such successful, loving people."

His kind words were her undoing, and she sniffled as she hugged him.

"Sunday would have loved your young man. Like to think the two of them might have picked up their guitars and played us both a fine song."

She laughed through her tears. "I would've loved to hear that."

"Instead, I don't have a doubt she's singing along in heaven. Probably knows all the words to Hunter's songs by now."

"Les keeps threatening to retire in a few years. He wants me to take over managing Mom and Dad, as well as Hunter."

"Sounds like a lot of work. Sure you're up to it?"

Ailis shook her head. "No, I'm sure I'm not."

Pop Pop frowned. "Now, Ailis—"

She held up her hand. "Not because I don't think I'm capable. But because Hunter and I want to start a family."

Pop Pop's smile grew wide. "Did you tell Les that?"

"Not yet."

"Lead with that. Guarantee you the man will work until he's a hundred if it means you'll bring babies into his world. Always sort of felt like you and Fiona got an extra uncle with Les in your lives, not that you didn't have enough to begin with."

"That's good advice. I'll make sure to pass my plans for the future along to him."

Pop Pop took her hand and gave it a squeeze. "Always knew you'd do great things, my beautiful witch."

She laughed as she kissed him on the cheek before whispering in his ear, "Boo!"

Mari Carr

Enjoy Wild Desire?

Please consider leaving a review.

Mari Carr

Enjoy Wild Desire?

Please consider leaving a review.

ABOUT THE AUTHOR

Writing a book was number one on Mari Carr's bucket list. Now her computer is jammed full of stories — novels, novellas, short stories and dead-ends. A *New York Times* and *USA TODAY* bestseller, Mari finds time for writing by squeezing it into the hours between 3 a.m. and daybreak when her family is asleep.

You can visit Mari's website at www.maricarr.com. She is also on Facebook and Twitter.

Titles by Mari Carr

Big Easy:
Blank Canvas
Crash Point
Full Position
Rough Draft
Triple Beat
Winner Takes All
Going Too Fast

Boys of Fall:
Free Agent
Red Zone
Wild Card

Trinity Masters:
Elemental Pleasure
Primal Passion
Scorching Desire
Forbidden Legacy
Hidden Devotion
Elegant Seduction
Secret Scandal
Delicate Ties
Beloved Sacrifice
Masterful Truth

Masters' Admiralty:
Treachery's Devotion
Loyalty's Betrayal
Pleasure's Fury
Honor's Revenge
Bravery's Sin

Compass:
Northern Exposure
Southern Comfort
Eastern Ambitions
Western Ties
Winter's Thaw
Hope Springs
Summer Fling
Falling Softly
Heaven on Earth
Into the Fire
Still Waters
Light as Air

June Girls:
No Recourse
No Regrets

Just Because:
Because of You
Because You Love Me
Because It's True

Lowell High:
Bound by the Past
Covert Affairs
Mad about Meg

Second Chances:
Fix You
Dare You
Just You
Near You
Reach You
Always You

Sparks in Texas:
Sparks Fly
Waiting for You
Something Sparked
Off Limits
No Other Way
Whiskey Eyes

What Women Want:
Sugar and Spice
Everything Nice

Cocktales:
Party Naked
Screwdriver
Bachelor's Bait
Screaming O

Wild Irish:
Come Monday
Ruby Tuesday
Waiting for Wednesday
Sweet Thursday
Friday I'm in Love
Saturday Night Special

Any Given Sunday
Wild Irish Christmas

Wilder Irish:
Wild Passion
Wild Desire
Wild Devotion
Wild at Heart
Wild Temptation
Wild Kisses
Wild Fire
Wild Spirit

Individual Titles:
Seducing the Boss
Tequila Truth
Erotic Research
Rough Cut
Happy Hour
Power Play
Assume the Positions
Slam Dunk

Made in the USA
Coppell, TX
07 June 2022

78547782R00142